The Journey Times

To
All My Readers

Contents

Papla

One : 'How long will it take to reach Delhi?'

Rachpal: 'Sir, just three hours.'

One: 'Why? Your taxi seems to be brand new. The road is so smooth; nor is there any traffic.'

Rachpal: 'Sir, now the police has placed hidden cameras all along the highway to monitor speeding vehicles. They post you the bill; either pay up or face sittings in the court. My taxi owner will fire me from the job for such a misadventure,' he cackled.

The boy suddenly applied the break, the taxi screeched and stopped. A cool and casual bull was crossing the highway. Rachpal hurled abuses at him. The amused bull flicked his tail and continued undisturbed.

Rachpal: 'Look at this idiot. My Papla is far more sober and disciplined.'

One: 'Who is Papla? Your son?'

Rachpal grinned, 'I am not married yet. I will be marrying next month, a day after my younger sister's marriage.'

One: 'How old are you?'

Rachpal: 'Twenty-one.'

One: 'Your sister?'

Rachpal: 'Sixteen.'

They kept quiet for a while.

Rachpal broke the silence, 'I am worried, who will look after Papla once she goes to her husband.'

One: 'Who is Papla?'

Rachpal: 'He is my bullock. He is just two years old, still a baby. He is growing up very well.'

One: 'You said that he is unlike the other one we came across?'

Rachpal: 'Yes, Papla is very bright and cheerful. Never does a stupid thing like crossing a highway. Sir, he lives in our village home and never goes out alone.'

One: 'How big is your house?'

Rachpal: 'It is quite big. We have six rooms amidst half an acre of compound, surrounded by a henna hedge and a wall at places. Papla lives near the main gate of the compound. We do not tie him up. In the winter he lives inside, in a room, next to my mother's. He has his own bed and quilt. He is very clever; he never dirties it unless unwell.'

One: 'In case he soils his bed then who cleans his dung?'

Rachpal: 'My mother and sister.'

One: 'And you?'

Rachpal: 'I stay in the city, and drive a taxi to make money. My mother manages the farm. These days agriculture does not pay, so I earn the money here and send my savings to her. My youngest brother goes to school, he is only ten.'

Both fell silent. The passenger dozed off. Rachpal waited to tell him more about Papla. On a clear stretch of road, he shouted,

'Are you sleeping, Sir?'

'No, I had just closed my eyes. Were you saying something?' The passenger became alert.

Rachpal: 'We do not use Papla for ploughing, Sir. He is like a member of our family. When I go to the village, Papla can smell me from 600 yards, and calls out affectionately. Whenever I chat with my village buddies, out of hearing range of my family members, Papla quietly listens to us; he moos across the hedge wall, wanting to join us. He always wants to follow me.'

One: 'Hmm.'

Rachpal: 'He affectionately licks all the family members—me on my face. No thief can enter our compound. Papla recognises bad people and chases them.'

One yawned, closed his eyes, and asked, 'If you do not use a bullock for ploughing, what utility has it? He only eats up your money.'

Rachpal became somewhat defensive. 'It is a racing bullock, Sir. Ever since I was a baby, I had wanted a racing bullock.

'For the want of an ox, our farm yield suffered. We used to hire oxen for our fields, but it is always difficult to get them during the sowing season. Three years ago, I became a taxi driver, and had saved seven-thousand rupees for an ox. A village elder was going to Hissar, the largest cattle market in North India and so I gave him all my money and asked him to bring a small calf of the best breed. A full-grown ox is very expensive. Moreover, they are un-teachable. We thought of raising the calf ourselves. This uncle got Papla for only five thousand rupees. Papla was six months old, then. He is such a lively and playful boy, that I have vowed never to put him under the yoke. Ploughing reduces a lively ox to a dull animal. My mother was annoyed at my decision, but she relented; it meant considerable labour for her at home and on the farm. But, Sir, you know the greatness of Indian women. How they voluntarily suffer for the happiness of their children?' Rachpal marvelled at Indian women.

One felt irritated at his selfishness. He wryly asked, 'You haven't spoken about your father?'

Rachpal: 'Sir, he died when I was nine years old. He, too, was very fond of bullock racing. My mother has brought us up single-handedly. She is a very courageous woman.'

One: 'I see. I am sorry to hear of yours father's untimely death. It was, indeed, too early to go. But life is like that,' One philosophised. Rachpal paid no attention to One's condolences.

Rachpal said, 'Sir, there was a tournament in a neighbouring village. I took my spirited Papla to it. Papla ran so well that some strangers came to me and offered me fifteen-thousand rupees for him. I flatly rejected the temptation, no second thoughts about it. Papla is like a brother to me. Every month I take leave from my master and go to my village to see Papla. He is shaping so well, and is very handsome. People are envious of him. My sister ties rakhi to him. Sir, he is a real brother to all of us.

'Papla drinks five 'kilograms' of milk every day, from his stone bowl. He is fed five big rotis made of five cereals: gram, jowar, bajra, corn and wheat. The rotis are dipped in pure ghee—only then does he eat them. He is quite finicky about his food.'

One: 'What else does he eat?'

Rachpal: 'He also eats hay.'

One: 'What about greens?'

Rachpal: 'We do not give him greens. They bloat his stomach.'

One: 'You must give him vitamins, too. Ask a doctor, whether not giving him green fodder is all right.'

Rachpal: 'What are vitamins?'

He applied the break again. This time he had spotted a large white and grey cow, and told One that his Papla was four inches taller than the cow. They stopped to look at the cow. She flicked her tail in contempt, and turned around.

One: 'Is Papla the same colour?'

Rachpal: 'Yes. But he is much thinner. He is very thin.'

One: 'I f he is so thin, does he not get exhausted during racing?'

Rachpal: 'Oh, no! Never! He runs like a deer. He is very agile and has solid muscles. His coat shines. My brother massages him every other day with a handful of grass.'

One: 'Which grass?'

Rachpal: 'Doob grass is the best. It is fibrous and does not have much juice in it.'

One: 'How many races has he won?'

Rachpal: 'Many, Sir. When he was ten months old he ran with giants and crossed the track in forty-one seconds. No one could beat him, except the four bullocks who joined at the end. They were all four and five years old. Papla was the youngest among the twenty participants. Papla ranked fifth in the race. My maternal uncle had also come to our house, and gone with us to the tournament. He announced a special prize for Papla—it was five-hundred rupees. After the prize was announced, many people showed an interest in Papla and one man offered me eighty-thousand for him. As I told you, I told him, too, that Papla is a brother to me. I will never sell him. He tried to feed Papla some bananas. Papla charged and the man ran for his life, cursing.'

'Ha, ha, ha, ha.' Both laughed imagining the scene created by Papla. Rachpal continued hysterically. One admonished him to be careful while driving.

Rachpal: 'Sorry, Sir. I am really very sorry. Sir, Papla never accepts food from strangers.'

One: 'But now that Papla is two years old, has he won any tournament?'

Rachpal: 'Several, Sir. He is among the first five bullocks in the Punjab these days. He has already won us over two lakhs. Someone has offered four lakhs for Papla. But I have told you already that I can not sell a brother.'

One: 'Four lakhs! That is more than the price of a new car. I could never imagine that much for a bullock.'

Rachpal: 'Four lakhs are nothing. There is a bullock in Ludhiana. He is number one in the Punjab. He is undefeatable. Do you know the price his new owner paid?'

One: 'No. What was that?'

Rachpal: 'Eight lakhs.'

Rachpal laughed at One's naivety. One was stunned. He kept quiet.

They entered the city limits of Delhi. The highway had

become crowded. Rachpal had become careful. Cars and trucks zoomed past recklessly. One has to be cautious while driving in Delhi. No one follows the rules of the road. Even the police jeeps cross at a red light. Although you may drive correctly, a careless driver may hit your car in an instant.

One asked a few more questions. Rachpal had become quieter and cautious. On reaching his destination, One paid off Rachpal, who promised to give One a CD on Papla; One promised to copy it and return it safely to Rachpal. They shook hands, exchanged telephone numbers. One promised that next time, too, he would call Rachpal for a trip outside Delhi.

Six months later, One found Rachpal's card. One had to visit another town again. He was reminded of Papla. Rachpal had not sent him the CD. He called Rachpal to bring his taxi. Rachpal arrived. His taxi was as tip-top as it had been the first time. Rachpal looked thinner, paler and subdued this time, not at all cheerful. He wore a turban and looked more mature. One congratulated Rachpal on the twin marriages in the family—Rachpal's and his sister's.

Rachpal smiled feebly and thanked him.

'Are you not happy?' One asked.

'I'm, I am happy.'

An awkward silence followed. Rachpal negotiated through a crowded turn.

'How is Papla?'

Rachpal laughed painfully, 'Oh, you still remember him. I am trying to forget him.'

'Why? What is the matter, Rachpal?' One appeared concerned.

Rachpal's mother had become very sick. Her intestine was obstructed, and she was in great agony. The village doctor advised her to go to a town and seek medical attention. Her sons took her to Ludhiana in a bus. The surgeons decided to operate.

There was no one left at home to look after Papla. Rachpal's sister came and took Papla to her husband's home. The husband assured his wife that he would look after their beloved Papla. She kissed her third brother goodbye. Now carefree, she took a bus to Ludhiana to be with her mother and brothers.

She cooked meals for them outside the hospital compound under a neem tree. The siblings stayed and slept in the open, with the relatives of the other admitted patients. They would see their mother, when allowed. Their mother had developed an infection in her wound. It took some time for her to recover.

Rachpal's brother-in-law took a dislike to the pampered Papla. In the absence of his wife, he treated Papla like an ill-bred beast. This man was too lazy to cook Papla's feast. Papla felt forlorn and heartbroken. He got into the bad habit of running away from his new home, wandering and eating garbage.

The siblings were still at the hospital, attending to their convalescent mother. One day, the brother-in-law came to the hospital and broke the news that their unruly beast was run over by a truck on the highway, some time at night.

Rachpal's eyes became moist. Rachpal had brought the CD in case One still remembered Papla. Rachpal took the CD out from the dashboard and handed it to One. He told One, 'Sir it is a gift to you. Do not copy and return it. Keep it with you.'

□

The Spooky House of Murari

Our medical school was in a backward district of a backward state of India. The school, actually, was unqualified to be called a medical school. Yet, it was an accredited school. Local medical practitioners taught there on a part-time basis. Since these doctors practised, they often missed taking their classes, and therefore encouraged self-learning by the students. The nurses in the medical school's hospital left by noon to work in private clinics and surgeries. The school hospital never had any bandages, life-saving drugs, facilities for investigations, or patients. Out of a thousand beds, the hospital never had more than fifty occupied at any given time. The citizens complained to the government. The government imposed a ban on private practice by the professors. The ministry raised funds for the hospital. But, still, the hospital remained what it was; it never improved. The senior officer in the ministry embezzled all the grants given to the college. More grants to improve the college meant only greater embezzlement. The doctors paid hefty bribes to the police, bureaucrats and the health and police ministers to continue their practice outside the school's hospital.

Professor Murari Lal, I am not sure if he is still alive, was a physiology teacher in the medical school. He was a good-natured man and was poorer than the others since he could not manage private practice. He had lost touch with medicine because patients never figured in his specialisation. He lacked initiative, too. He was scared of wrongdoing and bribing. He, along with his chief, was once suspended on charges of corruption. The chief bribed the Secretary in the government and resumed his duties. Murari remained in doubt about the Secretary's integrity for two years. Finally, trusting him to be dishonest, he borrowed thirty-five thousand rupees from the bank and paid the Secretary's footman. The charges were dropped, and he could resume his job again.

As his son could not be admitted to the medical course, he sent him to the Ukraine for education, where, admission was easier and the costs lower. There, just show your 12th pass certificate, deposit roubles, learn their language for a year, join the medical course and become a doctor in seven years. Murari's son spent ten years in the Ukraine. He got a wife, two children and a divorce decree, but not any medical degree. Neither did he visit his parents once, nor did he return a penny to them. Murari had accrued a huge debt on account of his son's education. Being a good-natured man, he never let his disappointments show. He always spoke pleasantly. His other son was a successful psychotherapist and helped his father out of his financial morass.

The house Murari lived in was strange. Several things were spooky over there. God only knows why he practised the magic therapy. He learnt the art from reki and pranik healers. Over a period of time his practice shadowed the best of physicians in the town, though he charged a pittance, sometimes only blessings.

A grateful patient presented Murari with a heifer. Though sickly, the heifer appeared to be of a good breed. The veterinarian treated the heifer and she grew up to become a beautiful and healthy cow. She was very friendly and fond of the family members. Murari affectionately called her Nandini.

Five thousand years ago, Nandini was the magical cow of sage Vashistha. When King Vishwamitra wanted to abduct her by force, the magical creatures born out of the cow mauled and defeated the king's army. He had to retreat empty-handed.

The cow was a divine gift to the family. They kept her well-fed in their courtyard. A man was employed to give her long walks. In due course, Nandini delivered a healthy calf, and produced ten litres of milk each day. However, Murari was disappointed as his neighbour's superior bred cow gave twenty litres each day. By the end of the year, Nandini dried up. It was the beginning of June, the hottest month in North India. Hot air sprayed dust over the cities, villages, roads, houses and the foliage. The whole environment became extremely dusty.

People drink tea to pass time and overcome boredom. It becomes an addiction. Tea just flows in middle-class Indian homes. Each guest is offered a cup of sweet milky tea, and the host offers him company. But, getting a regular supply of pure milk in towns is always a problem. During the extremely hot summer months, often, the cattle dry up, and the supply of milk is insufficient. These are the trying times in Indian homes. The milkmen always add water before they sell the milk. This diluted milk then loses its flavour and one has to add a lot of it to the tea. Sometimes the tea needs to be cooked in this kind of milk. Powdered milk is always the last resort for the Indian palate.

The pandit had fixed the 30th of June for the wedding of Murari's daughter. The Municipal Corporation had banned the production of milk sweets to meet the shortage of milk in the town. But the milk was still not there. The guests began arriving at Murari's house. He had difficulty offering milky tea to his guests. It had become a question of Murari's honour. More guests arrived the following night. Tea could not be served since there was no milk.

Nandini stood silently in the yard licking her year-old calf. Murari looked at her soulfully. The cow mooed inviting him to massage her neck. Murari massaged her neck and bowed to her ear. He plainly told her his difficulty and begged her to help. He reminded her of Vashistha's Nandini. Nandini affectionately licked his palm. He again patted her and returned to the guests.

In the evening, Nandini was uncomfortable. She kicked her hind legs into the air and mooed loudly. Murari went to calm her and said endearing words. Murari was surprised to notice that her udders were engorged and her teats were flushed. A drop of milk had oozed out of a teat. Tears rolled out of Murari's eyes. He was an emotional man. He kissed Nandini's forehead in gratitude. Thereafter, there was no dearth of milk for tea in Murari's house till the last guest departed. Nandini dried up again till she delivered her next calf.

If you believe in magic, Nandini was indeed a magical cow. If you are a rationalist, you may simply call her an intelligent animal, for she never stopped helping her master's family.

The whole family used to sleep in their one and only air-conditioned room. They would lock and seal the room from the inside to avoid the hot wind. The electrical wiring of the house was old and of a low standard, not unusual with government houses. The next summer, somewhere along the electrical cable, a short-circuit caused fire in the house at midnight. The flames spread all over. The family, unaware of the destruction outside, slept cosily inside. All of a sudden, they were woken by a terrible noise outside the door. Someone was trying to break in violently. They were frightened. They thought the dacoits had come. They did not open the door. The noise at the door became louder, till finally the door fell apart. Nandini entered the room; smoke and fire followed her. One of Nandini's horns was broken, she was bleeding. The house was an inferno. All of them ran out along with Nandini and her calf.

She had saved them that night. They thanked her from the bottom of their hearts.

That was not the end of their luck. Small, eerie incidents always kept happening to them. I will tell you of another real story that I heard about their house. There was an old mango tree within their courtyard. Several occupants over the last twenty years had lived in the house. Never once, had any of them seen a mango hanging from that tree. That year, the horticulture superintendent of the area visited the campus houses. He noted the bad reputation of this tree. He offered to have it cut down, and plant another instead. Murari agreed. Winter is not the best season to cut down trees; so they decided to do it the following March. Murari had got time to heal the tree. He tried his magic recipes, that he had learnt to cure barren women, on the mango tree. He spoke to the soul of the tree.

In February, the tree turned white with fragrant blossoms. In March, for the first time, its branches were full of green mangoes. Parrots nested in it. The horticulture superintendent did not believe his eyes when he saw the tree in bloom. After the surprised man had left, Murari embraced and whispered to the mango tree, 'My brother, I will never cut you down. You need not bear any fruit as long as I live in this house. Be happy. Feel free. I will never cut you down.' He kissed the tree on a leaf.

□

Patience

He was a clerk in the city post office. To make ends meet, he used to work in a photography shop in the evenings. He was a good photographer. Once the children grew up, his responsibilities were over; he retired to his village, far from the city. Surrounded by green hills, it was a small village of a few hundred houses. The old man lived with his wife on his pension and savings.

He always wanted to own a camera to record the ordinary as well as extraordinary moments of his life. He wanted to capture the river, the crops, the buffaloes, unknown urchins, the market and everything else in his village on print, for posterity. He always had regretted, not having saved the lost glories on his camera—the steam engines, horse carriages, fashion in his youth and weirdly dressed men and women at village fairs. The blue green butterflies that hovered everywhere during the day, and the glow-worms which silhouetted the trees at night, were not there any more. The centuries-old Shiva temple along with its beautiful idol had vanished. People would never know the history of the mound in its place. Girls then, were old women now. No proof of their youth was available. Once upon a time, his boyhood friends still living in the village, looked handsome, strong and taller—a fact unbelievable today. Many of them had no photographs of their youth. Some of them had even died without leaving any trace of their existence. He feared that the same might happen to the contemporary landscape and people.

Photography was his ideal of service to his village. He became increasingly obsessed with the idea. The camera became a pressing necessity of his life.

He discussed his desire with his old employer, the photographer in the city. Sometimes, unused second-hand cameras were sold to the photographer for further sale. The old man always arrived a few days late; the camera would be sold out. The photographer always counselled patience.

Years passed. The digitals had arrived in the market.

A visit to the city was not an easy affair; one had to plan the event well in advance, may be three to four months. The old man scanned the advertisements for the new cameras in the newspapers and magazines. He noted their specifications and prices. Whenever he went to the city, he discovered to his amazement that the cameras he had selected had become cheaper by a quarter. For the same price, cameras with superior functions were available. The shop assistants, instead of helping him out to settle for a camera, always confused him. He would return with a pile of new brochures. He would read the fresh material, and underline the points to be clarified during his next visit to the city.

He studied cameras for almost a decade without arriving at any decision. Meanwhile, many more things faded and disappeared. Moustaches and beards went out of fashion; the boys in the village grew long hair, and the girls dressed like men. He too had grown older and frailer. His eyes troubled him, his hands shook and the joints creaked. He still passionately looked for a camera in the newspapers and magazines.

One day, a courier agent brought a parcel to him. His own grandson had sent it. He cut open the packet. A tiny silvery thing slipped out of it. He had a camera in his hand for the first time in the twenty years after his retirement. His heart uncontrollably fluttered in excitement. He did not know how to use the instrument; it was a knobless, smooth, little thing. The delivery boy, though in a hurry, stopped to teach him. The old man rushed to call his wife. The delivery boy snapped them in different poses. The pictures of the couple were stored in the camera. The pictures came obediently to the screen, and when asked, disappeared in memory. The old man's glee knew no bounds. He asked the postman to shoot the dusty brown moth on the white wall, his dog, close-up of his hands. Everything was so professional! The result was instantaneously visible. The delivery boy patiently taught him the basics. The boy was in a hurry, he had to deliver letters and parcels. He promised to come again.

The old man's hands were unsteady, but the photographs were brilliant as if shot by a professional camera, mounted on a tripod. His joy knew no limit, he ran to the market, rice field, the river, the village school, and the railway track, and effortlessly took wonderful photographs. Unlike the old days, no developing was required. He showed his photographs to his friendly neighbours. They were impressed. Later, he photographed all the functions in the village, the school drill, marriages, family celebrations and festivals. The man at the cybercafé stored his images on the CDs. The old man ran clicking all over.

But his joy did not last long. The very third month, he discovered an advertisement for a superior model at the price of his camera. He felt cheated, and wished for some more wisdom and patience in his grandson. He wrote admonishing his grandson for his mindless haste, 'I waited for almost ten years. Could you not wait for even three months? Patience is a great virtue, my son.'

□

Life is Beautiful

Danville is a small town in California, perhaps southeast to the Bay—I may be wrong. One can see undulating hills over the area. The hills covered with trees and bushes appear like crinkled and curly hair on the head of an African, with bald patches in between. My host lived in a beautiful cottage over a hill. There are several cottages in the development area occupied by affluent Americans and successful immigrants. I was surprised to see wild peacocks there. Perhaps, some Asian had left them over there? But then, during twilight hours, I observed fearful deer running across our backyard. They were surely native; no one could hide their eggs and carry them from Asia.

Closing my surgery, away from the summer of India, I had a full month to enjoy life in the US. The host, my sister, would leave early for her work and would return late. That is the way to make money to be able to live in the exquisite isolation of Danville amidst the sparse crowd of millionaires. I would have died of boredom had I not discovered Black Hawk Plaza, a two-mile walk, on another hill.

The plaza had a car museum. The ticket cost only one dollar. An idler informed me that one could spend the whole day sleeping on the benches inside. There was a movie hall, surgery of a plastic surgeon, beautiful curios, arts and utility shops and of course several restaurants along a small artificial river running on pumped water. Ducks, fishes, rocks and weeping willows alongside the edge of the river gave it a natural look.

To my amazement, I found only a few people making use of the place. Mostly, the young mothers with their small children spent time in the riverside restaurants. I always wondered, to whom these shops sold their goods.

To closely observe the life and behaviour of the American people, I used to visit the place at noon and sometimes read a book on a bench. An ice cream or a cup of coffee ensured my right to use a restaurant's chair indefinitely. I suspect that the parlour man welcomed me. He probably felt a false sense of fullness and popularity of his joint. Once he fed me a cone of ice cream at his own cost. Americans are honest with money. Nothing is for free, they proclaim. I believe that the ice cream compensated for my service to his shop; my presence was an advertisement for his empty shop. In fact, once an indecisive man watching me slurping my coffee entered the shop, and ordered a cup for himself.

I photographed every bit and corner of his shop. Americans love wild and funny ideas. I told him that I was seriously considering becoming a travel-writer. Once he learnt of my interest, he helped me to photograph the neighbouring establishments as well. They do not openly differentiate between a reputed and not-yet-promising author. An excellent attitude, it helped me; I must admit.

Once I was passionately engaged in a discussion on the food habits of Californian quails, with an old woman. A young South Asian lady, with a walkie-talkie in hand, passed by me and smiled. I immediately lost interest in the old lady and quails, and also her little dog. With age, women become clairvoyants unlike men of the same age. The old woman remembered some urgent task and left. The restaurateur, without my asking, told me that the lady who passed by was an Indian, and in the security department. Like a Good Samaritan he gave her a call to meet 'a budding author' from India. After a while the girl reappeared smiling. We sat at the table by the riverside, under a rainbow umbrella, and with coffee this time.

She was a pretty and small woman with a pronounced North Indian accent, something very rare. It is a saying in India: those who once fly over the US, even if they do not actually land there, acquire a Yankee accent for life. The woman had a soft and friendly face. She did not seem highly educated, perhaps a college drop-out.

Not averse to flirtation, I smiled, 'Samita is a nice name. Easy for Americans to pronounce.'

'Rahul is better.' She complimented me.

'How did you land here?' I asked

'I came on a fiancé visa.'

'Oh I see, so you are married.'

'And you?'

'I am single, a divorcee.'

'I am not married.'

'Then? You came on a fiancé visa, did you?'

'Oh!' She sighed. 'All that is very painful to recollect. I did come here on a fiancé visa, but never got married.'

'Why?'

'I came with many dreams. My fiancé! I met him through marriage dot com. We fixed our marriage through the internet. He visited India for the engagement. My widowed mother was very pleased that after a rough patch I would be happy again. My son too liked him.'

'You have a son?'

'Yes. He is eleven. I am a divorcee. My son stays with my brother, back home in Karnal.'

Karnal is a small town near Delhi.

'I know! I know! I have been there.' I was amazed at her enterprise.

'I came here. Sunil came to the airport with a Fijian woman

to receive me. She was beautiful, charming and very classy. I feared, lest my man should fall in love with her. After an hour's drive, we got home. My fiancé showed me a comfortable room, all to myself. I deposited my luggage and went to sleep. I admired my fiancé's sense of chastity. We would share the room only after we got married. I sincerely liked the purity of the man. He was a handsome man, so pure in heart, I thought.' Her face sagged, her eyes became moist.

'Please continue. I am noting, I will write your story.' She looked surprised. I completed, 'Only if you permit. Of course, I will change your name so that no one can recognise you.' I looked at her.

'Certainly, you may write my story, if that helps your career.'

'The next morning Sunil woke me up. He arrived with a tray of tea and laid it on the table. He drew the curtains to let sunshine in. I was still groggy. It was night for me by the Indian time. He smiled, and told me to relax and went away. He was so kind, unlike other Indian men. I was pleased.

'I got up, had a bath and felt fresh. I sipped the cold tea and came out. There was nobody in sight in the family room. Upstairs I could hear the sound of TV. I climbed up, the door was lightly closed. I pushed to open it. Sunil and Jainti were lying on the same bed and watching TV. I reflexly closed the door and ran down the staircase. Sunil came after me. He looked embarrassed. I turned my face away. I heard him, "Jainti is a close friend, she lives with me. She has no objection to our marriage. But she will stay with us."

'I was crying. He tried to console me. Jainti also spoke to me very kindly and tried to convince me of the arrangement. We went out in the evening to look around. I cried whenever I could.'

She stopped to wipe the corner of her eye. I had become impatient to hear such interesting gossip.

'Then?'

She understood my impatience, and smiled. She looked at

her watch. 'This is how we lived for a week. He allowed me to telephone my family in India. To them, I said pleasant things about my life here. The truth would have killed my mother.

'One afternoon, when he was away at work, I stole his dollar bills and left 'home' without informing them. I had found a BART station where many homeless people lived.

'The people who lived there looked ferocious and criminal, but I preferred them to my *own home*. They were drug addicts, mentally challenged and old people. I lived with them. They fed me. I lived there unwashed for a few months, and begged for alms. Indians shooed me away. I wanted to talk to them and ask for help. They thought I was a drug addict and a beggar, and looked away in disgust when I said "halloji," "bhaisaheb" or "behenji" to them.

'The US is an organised country. You cannot hide for long. One day a policeman discovered me, and asked for my papers. He ordered me to follow him quietly. On my way, a kind Indian lunged at me, and talked to me in Hindi. He passed a card to me. It was an Indian lawyer's business card. The man said that the lawyer would help me. "Show them this card. Tell them that you know this lawyer. Speak to the police only in Hindi."

'I was too scared. At the police station they sent me for a bath. I was sent to a hospital for a checkup. There I rang up Papaji.'

'Now, who is this Papaji?' I asked.

'I call Mr Bhimani, Papaji. He is a lawyer. He came to the police station. I told him all about my misery. He asked me to tell the police that I was his relative. Papaji organised my release. I had no place to go. Papaji and his wife asked me to move in with them, so that I could have an address to fight against deportation.

'Papaji fought and won the battle for me. The court has allowed me to continue here. Even today, I do not understand all the legal details.

'I always lied to my mother saying that I was so happy here.

One day, my brother informed me that my mother had passed away. She was happy for me till her end. My son is also very pleased at his mother's luck. He always asks me, "When will you call me, mummy?" I always tell him that it will be very soon. He is the only centre of my life, now.'

'How did you get this job?' I asked.

'Papaji's daughter, who is my age, has helped me. Now I get here by eight o'clock in the morning and stay till four.'

'Are you free after 4 today? Shall we go out for dinner tonight?' I suggested.

'No Uncleji, I have to reach Mummyji's 9-11 Store. I work there till midnight,' she said sternly.

I felt dressed down by her address. I wondered how she had come to know of my age. I always thought I looked fifteen years younger than my fifty-five.

'But you can come to me at Walnut Creek on Wednesday afternoon. That is my off time.' This time she smiled.

I felt relieved.

'How much money do you make, if I may ask?' The Indian in me slyly woke up.

'I make three to four thousand dollars a month. I live in a room in Papaji's house. I save some money so that my son can come and join me here. I wish to educate him here. He should become a well-educated man.'

I calculated that this girl was not sleeping more than five hours a day. She cooked her dinner after midnight, got up early to prepare her breakfast and lunch for the day.

'Uncleji, you must try to settle here. It is never late. Life is so good here. Now I have purchased a second hand sports car. It is ten years old. It will become antique one day and fetch me a lot more money.' She smiled in blissful ignorance. 'What is there in India to waste one's life on? I tell you, there is one Deputy Superintendent of Police from Ludhiana, now he works here.'

'Deputy SP is an important position. So many people salute

him in India. What does he do here?'

'He has his sister here. His brother-in-law sponsored him here. He joined the hospitality industry when he came.'

'What is the hospitality industry?' I naively asked.

'He worked as a waiter in McDonalds and Burger King. But here, there is a natural system of *hiring and firing*. It is not derogatory as we believe it to be in India. This happens to everybody here.'

'Oh, I see. What does he do now?'

'Now, he is in housekeeping. He is a janitor.'

We have no *janitors* in India, therefore I could not comprehend. I looked blank. She understood my ignorance of the term. 'Janitors are the people who clean toilets,' she clarified.

She dispelled my astonishment, 'Here, there is tremendous dignity of labour. Everyone is equally respected. No one is big or small here. I use my boss' first name and talk to him as an equal.

'Initially the Deputy SP was very status conscious. He felt disappointed taking up this assignment. But that actually helped him with his Green Card. When he went for his interview, they asked him, "What do you do?" He literally barked, "I clean your shit." They burst into a roar. Would you believe it? They congratulated him then and there for winning his Green Card.

'Why don't you also try your luck here? Your sister is here. You have family support. I say, it is never late.' She giggled innocently.

I had nothing to say; I cooed and mooed incoherently and took her leave.

□

Realisation of Illusion

The Princess was the darling of her father, the King. Parental indulgence had made her obstinate and tyrannical. Before the words flew off her lips, her wish was to be fulfilled—at all costs, by all means. The servants understood what she desired and what was to be done to please her, much before she actually spoke.

The King found a young husband for his little Princess in a distant land, a thousand miles away. The princess of Thar was married to the King of Chatpatpur.

The Queen—the princess was a queen now, found Chatpatpur quite weird and uncivil. The people spoke a strange dialect, and had stranger traditions and manners. They took a lot of time to understand their queen; sometimes they asked for an interpreter. The Queen never got used to the people of Chatpatpur, particularly the servants. She was dismayed to deal with them; she considered them dimwits and lazy. She actually had to explain her needs to them, clarify several times with gestures of hand and foot, and then only did they half- understand her. She was fed up with them.

The Queen decided to teach them a lesson and show them that she did not give two hoots for them, and that she was not dependent on them. She decided to do her chores with her own hands and be self-reliant.

It was the first day of her resolve. The Queen shouted, 'Thapo Bai. Bring a stove here. Quick, quick.' Thapo Bai ran to fetch the stove. The Queen had never asked her to do these errands, for she never worked in the kitchen. Confused, she ran to the kitchen, and fumbled around till the cook passed her the stove. The Queen shouted to another maid, 'O lazy woman, don't shirk your duties all the time, come here. Bring some coal and a matchbox. Fast!'

Mohun's wife brought the coal and wood shavings. She quickly set the coal pieces in the oven, put up a dressing of wood shavings and set them on fire. She blew the air with a bamboo pipe. The coal soon began smouldering.

'Have you washed and cut the vegetables, O dim mistress of Ganesh?'

'Huzoor, I am Paltu's wife.'

'I know all about you.' The Queen glared at her and shouted, 'Wash and cut the vegetables. Don't forget to bring some butter oil, salt and spices.' Paltu's wife darted like a headless hen straight to the kitchen.

The cook helped her with the materials, and she brought back the items. The Queen carefully inspected each piece of the chopped vegetables and smiled with satisfaction. 'Put the pot on fire, and pour a little oil in it.' Paltu's wife complied. The oil became hot. The Queen asked Paltu's wife to add the spices to the oil. The spices filled the room with an inviting aroma. Paltu's wife put the chopped vegetables into the pot before the Queen could ask for it. This angered the Queen. She snatched the ladle from the servant's hand and stirred the pot herself.

A new realisation dawned on her; she snorted, 'What a fool I was to depend on others to cook for me. Look ye, all the stupid men and women of Chatpatpur, I could do everything myself. I don't depend on you for anything. Henceforth, I will be independent of you.' The Queen rose triumphantly and left the ladle and the simmering pot.

Paltu's wife quietly took hold of the ladle before it could fall on the ground. The excited Queen ran to the King, and informed him about her resolve, and how she won her victory over the lazy servants.

Paltu's wife added water to the stew, stirred it, and put the lid on the pot. She sat there till the vegetable was cooked. She removed the pot from the fire and put the dish in a golden bowl. The other women in the kitchen had prepared other dishes, and chapattis. They laid all the preparations on the table for the royal couple to dine. The King opened the prominently displayed golden bowl, tasted it, and proclaimed that he had never tasted such an excellent dish ever before. Serving another portion, the Queen humbly blushed.

□

The Old Man Who Sold His House

An old couple owned a posh house in an upmarket area of Delhi. They seemed to be rich, but they were not. They had two sons; both were married and had children. All of them stayed together. The old man and his wife had the largest room of the house to themselves.

The man was a retired government servant. During the mid-1960s, when the price of real estate was down, he had bought a plot on Amrita Shergill Marg. On it, he constructed a double-storeyed house with his hard-earned money to live in comfort after his retirement. Now, a similar accommodation elsewhere, is a seven star luxury; Delhi is one of the most expensive cities in India.

This man was totally dependent on his wife. He could not even prepare a cup of tea for himself. They often discussed their impending departure from the world. The lady would often tell him, 'We will have to go one day. God knows who will leave first. It could be either you or me. It is not in our hands. You must learn to prepare tea by yourself and take care of yourself once I am gone.'

'Never say such things. I pray that I should go earlier. I won't survive once you leave,' the man would beg pathetically.

The woman prayed to God that the man should die before her. She knew that he would be miserable without her. When she could not bear her backache any more, they went to see a doctor. She was diagnosed as an advanced case of breast cancer. The cancer had spread to her spine and other organs too. The surgeon told the heartbroken couple that there was no hope for the lady. Still, the lady prayed to live longer than her husband. She made tea for him and fed him, till the time she could move. She managed to teach him to make tea for himself.

She was anxious about her old man. Before she died, she called her sons and asked them to look after their father well, as she did all her life. The sons promised their mother that they would look after their father, as well as she did all her life. One day she died peacefully leaving her husband to their sons.

The sons looked after their father as best as they could. Their own children were growing up, the space was becoming smaller. One day, the eldest son came to his father and humbly told him of his problem. Since the father did not need the biggest room any more, he suggested that they should exchange their rooms. The old man agreed. He did not need the room after his wife's death. He moved to a smaller room. Soon after, another grandson demanded a room to study; his examinations were approaching. The old man was yet again shifted to another room, the one over the garage.

This room was connected with the interior of the house, and a stairway led one to the lawn outside. His meals were sent to his room, alternately by his two sons. No one asked for him at the crammed dining table. The grandchildren were occupied with their school work at home, and had no time for the old man. One of his sons had installed a TV in his room so that he would not feel lonely and bored. The old man now felt completely disconnected with the family, and independent of them. He could come in and go out without having to come inside the house.

The old man fell sick for a few days, and no one in his family got to know about it. Meals were served in his room, and after a while the tray was removed by the servant. No one noticed that the old man was not eating. He recovered in due course.

His loneliness increased. He craved for human company. He would sit outside the gate and watch passers-by, count the number of cars that passed through the road, rush to greet the rich neighbours who seldom walked.

His children noticed his shabby clothes and appearance, and chided him. 'Haria does not listen to me. He says he has a lot of work and will do my laundry later. He hasn't washed my clothes for a month now.'

'Then wash your clothes yourself. Some work will be good for your health,' the elder son snapped at the old man. Haria, the household help, had found a job with better salary and less work. He had become a guard with a security agency. He quit the old man's house. The old man was now asked to help out and share the chores which he had never learnt or performed earlier. He was clumsy.

His blood pressure, diabetes and toothache exacerbated. It became difficult for him to visit the doctor regularly for his checkups. His need for help became even greater than ever before. He could not afford a taxi each time. The doctor chided him. His glaucoma operation was again postponed as it was not convenient for his children and their families. He could not even read the newspaper and watch the television well. Even on the road he would miss the sight of cars coming towards him. He had to adjust his head each time to see properly.

The old man remembered his wife each passing moment. He became resentful of his children. Had he let the house out on rent he would have become a millionaire and fended for himself better. He felt that his life had become like a bleak winter.

That year, the summer was exceptionally hot. The family could not take the heat in Delhi. The families of the two brothers decided to spend their summer in Mussoorie, a hill station in the Himalayas. Deserted houses are not safe from burglars. Someone had to stay back to keep burglars away. Naturally, it was the grandfather's house, he must safeguard it. The old man agreed to stay back. He would have become a burden on the young people in Mussoorie. Anyway, they would not have taken him along on one or another pretext.

Beating the summer heat, the two families returned. The city had become pleasant with the onset of the monsoon. Showers greeted them at Connaught Circus on their way home. Trees looked washed and greener. They passed through several tree-lined streets and circles and felt good.

The taxi driver asked them for the exact number of the house, for no house existed at the expected site. They peeped out and were very surprised not to find their house at its place. They checked out again. The familiar houses and shops were still there but their own house was amiss.

Only the garage stood. They could recognise it. Some men under transparent plastic sheets were digging the ground and loading the rubble on a truck. The giant, cotton silk tree, cut neatly into slices, lay on the ground. The families were in utter shock and disbelief. Their eyes split wide, hearts spewed out of their mouths. They rushed to the man supervising the workers. The man coolly looked at them and said, 'Are you Mr Bharucha's sons? He has sold this house to me. He has moved to the Royal Pensioners Hotel. Please collect your luggage from this garage by tomorrow, we have to demolish this too.'

□

The Weaver Bird and the Monkey

A little weaver bird stayed busy the whole day. She collected straw and grass from all over the place, and fixed them on a grass cushion over the twig of a laburnum tree. She would stitch the fibres with her beak, pull and scratch them, and then lick the weave to even out the surface like an expert weaver on a loom. At the end of her session, she examined her work carefully, and softly felt each knot and protuberance with her feet; when satisfied, she flew off to bring in more of the raw material to expand her nest.

Opposite the laburnum, there was an old oak tree. It was huge. Its intertwining branches made a sort of platform. A reputed family of monkeys lived there. There was a father monkey with his harem of wives and many kids. He used to admire the industrious bird and her crib. They would exchange friendly glances.

One day, the bird pointed to a man's hut and asked the monkey why he was not making a house for himself? The monkey smiled, 'We do not waste our time on such foolish things. We are believers, and believe in God, the merciful.'

Winter months lay ahead. The bird was pregnant, she expected to lay and hatch eggs. The chicks would need warmth in winter.

And, just before the winter, her cosy nest was ready. Her house was a hanging basket of sorts, very pretty. She would swing on it and sing. In course of time, she laid eggs in her warm nest, and protectively sat over them.

The winter had set in. Cold had increased, the winds chilled the bones. But the bird felt no discomfort. She was warm and happy. She had stored enough food as well. She slept most of the time and went out when the sun shone.

The blizzards in the mountains further cooled the valley. Then, it started snowing. The monkeys shivered. They huddled together to keep each other warm. The smallest one caught a chill and became very sick. One night, the baby monkey lost its strength and grip and fell down. He died on the spot. The family cried and mourned. It was too cold; they again huddled together to save themselves from the biting cold.

To make matters worse, it rained and the temperatures dipped further. Ponds froze and the rain water turned into icicles. Over the tree, the monkeys groaned in cold.

The bird felt awful looking at them. She was a kind-hearted creature, and could not bear the pain of others. She was warm in her crib, but felt very unhappy on account of the misery of her neighbours. One day, she observed, that another junior in her neighbourhood suffered a frost bite. The poor fellow lost his toe. She did not know how to help them. She felt very uneasy with her own comfortable lifestyle.

One day, the sun shone in the valley. The snow had melted. The weather became warmer. She flew to her neighbours on the oak tree, and earnestly urged the father monkey, 'Brother, winter has not yet gone. It will certainly return by the night. Why don't you also make a shelter, while the sun shines? Collect some hay from the farmer's barn, and some wood. You can spread it and cover the young children and yourself too. I suffer watching you shivering.'

The old monkey became very angry with the bird's arrogant

speech. He shouted back, 'O non-believer heathen, enemy of God, what business have you to advise me? Keep your advice to yourself. Listen to me, O dirty bird, if you speak one word more, I will wring your neck and crumple your stinking sack.' The monkey bared its teeth in anger. The tearful bird said, 'But, my brother…' She could not complete what she had to say. The monkeys pulled her house down. They threw her nest and the hatchlings in the cold river and smirked and snorted meanly at her.

□

The Bridegroom

Chaman was desperate to find a bride for himself. He lived in London. He had emigrated to Britain to study engineering in the nineteen-seventies. After completing his studies he got a decent job in the metropolis. Everything an Indian would want was available in London. Living in this city was like living in homeland, but with comforts. The salary was good; the house was heated; the place was clean and there was no dust; a car, refrigerator, TV and washing machine were affordable; the quality of goods was excellent; phones worked; the transport was good; and the girls were well-fed, good-looking and forward. There were no poor and smelly people, shanties and filthy areas. Everyone was a sahib. He decided to settle there.

In course of time, he brought his parents and siblings to London. He helped educate his brothers and sisters, and married them into wealthy immigrant families. All of them happily settled in the city. In their togetherness, they never missed Dhola Maru, their home in the backwaters of India. They adapted well to the country of their adoption and lived comfortably. The elder brother still felt responsible for them.

Having ensured the well-being and happiness of his parents and siblings, he thought of his own marriage. A lot of time had elapsed; he was well past his prime. He thought like a mature man; he weighed the pros and cons of each action and calculated profit versus loss in each adventure. Though he admired modern women, and occasionally flirted with them, but for a wife he sought a traditional woman, committed to her husband's family.

Chaman had come across a few Indian girls in England but the relationships did not last long. They were far too westernised. They did not wish to lead a typical Indian life, so to say, with their in-laws breathing down their necks. In order to facilitate his marriage, his parents moved out of London to a small village. But even that did not bring him any luck.

He tried some live-in relationships; those failed. His parents had grown very old. It was now 2007, and he felt very nervous about his marriage prospects.

He advertised his desire on an Indian website. He wrote, 'A traditional Rajasthani Hindu male, 48 years, five foot ten inches, spiritual in nature, strictly vegetarian, settled in London, with a five figure income in British pounds, wants a convent-educated virgin, less than thirty-five years with fair looks and complexion, and with traditional Indian values to serve his old parents. No bars.'

He received a flood of letters. He spoke to several of them on the telephone, and finally zeroed in on one thirty-five-year-old. She had a sweet voice. Her accent was not phoney, and she was convent-educated for sure. She also claimed to be very spiritual. They began to converse on the phone. They talked every other day for hours. They talked of a common spiritual guru. It seemed to be a fairy-tale affair.

Chaman was certain that at last he had found his dream girl, and the girl too thought the same. Chaman dyed with care the few hairs he had on his scalp. He tried several colours, but L'Oreal number four gave the best results. It was lighter in hue than the charcoal black of cheap dyes. The softness of the dye gave a real youthful glow to his face. He got his facial skin cut and stretched by a plastic surgeon. He fancied the looks of a forty-year-old, not a day older. These days one cannot tell a man's age; young men look so old, and the older men sit over their age and look boyish.

Finally, they decided to meet. He took a flight to Delhi to meet this girl. The girl too was excited at the idea of meeting her Prince Charming. Chaman brought his eighty-seven-year-old mother, in case they decided to get married on the spur of the moment. He got his ailing mother dyed, manicured and pedicured. She ought to look reasonable, a mother of a forty-year-old, and not of a forty-eight-year-old man.

A girl's wedding is a major event in India. To get a well-settled groom without any dowry is a great fortune. The girl's grateful family including her uncles, aunts and cousins turned up at the airport to receive Chaman. He stayed in an expensive hotel. The girl was really charmed by the sophisticated and suave suitor. Everyone else in the family too liked him. Although he looked somewhat old to them, they thought that good family care and home-cooked meals would restore his sagging looks. The girl was indeed pretty, as pretty as he thought while talking to her on the telephone. She looked under thirty.

The two went out to the restaurants, temples and gardens of Delhi, watched movies and music concerts together, cooed sweet nothings to each other. They really had an enjoyable time and were impressed by each other.

Before leaving for a short visit to Rajasthan, Chaman asked the girl, 'Do you really love me?'

'Yes I do, my love.'

'Will you always love me?'

'Always!'

'Will you love me even when I grow old?'

'Why, I too will grow old with you.'

'Yes, love is a spiritual thing and not related to age. How old do you think I am?'

'I know it. It is there on the net.'

'Don't you mind the age difference?'

'No. You look so healthy and handsome. I love you.'

'I too believe that age is immaterial; it is the love that matters. My sister married a man twenty years older. They are still deeply in love. Would you love me even if you learn that I am a hundred years old and you, just fifteen?'

'What silly things you say!'

'Don't you bother about the age difference then?'

'I have said that at least a dozen times. I love you. That's all.'

Chaman always thought that a girl in love can't count the years. He was convinced now. It was the time to be truthful, the risk was minimal. He smiled and took out his driving licence and handed it over to the girl.

The girl looked at it and said, 'English people are very aesthetic. They make beautiful cards.' She returned the card.

'Have you read the card?'

'No, why?'

'My age is written on it.' He returned the card to the girl.

'Well you are fixated on age!' She grumbled and read where he pointed his finger on the card. She returned the card with a smile.

He again repeated, 'Read carefully and loudly.'

She read aloud, 'Sixty-one years on...'

Her face turned ashen. She looked very pale and sick. She said, 'I am not feeling well.'

'What happened?' Chaman became anxious. He called the waiter to bring some cold water.

'No, it is all right. I will be fine once I reach home.'

'Let us go to a doctor,' Chaman suggested.

'It is all right, I must go back,' she said feebly.

'Did you get this sort of thing earlier?'

She did not reply and rose with an effort. She walked out listlessly holding the banister. Chaman helped her out of the restaurant, hailed a taxi and she drove away.

At home she opened the computer, and again checked Chaman's website. His age was written clearly, it was forty-eight years. She wept.

A few hours later, Chaman rang up. She did not pick up the phone. The following day, Chaman called her at her office, several times. She let the buzzer go. At last, she wrote an SMS, 'It is over. Please do not call me again. Thanks.'

Chaman wondered about her affirmations, and asked himself, 'Should lovers count years?' He studied his advertisement and corrected it. '~~A traditional Rajasthani Hindu~~ An Indian male, ~~48~~ 61 years, five foot ten inches, spiritual in nature, ~~strictly vegetarian,~~ settled in London, with ~~five figure income in British pounds~~ modest income, wants to marry an ~~convent~~ educated ~~virgin~~ woman for companionship~~, less than thirty-five years with fair looks and complexion, and with traditional Indian values to serve his old parents~~. No bars.' He reread it, felt satisfied and posted it on the site.

□

Tomb-Touch Obituarer

Have you ever been to Pondicherry, in India? It lies on the East Coast facing the Bay of Bengal. In earlier times, it was a French colony. Still a number of residents speak French as their mother tongue. The influence of the European culture and architecture is visible all over. But never mind if you have not visited the place; its layout is geometric, and its map is easy to read.

Four houses northwards from the intersection of the Gandhi Road and Nehru Street, adjacent to the French Potatoes (a famous eatery), you will find a yellow building bearing an interesting board on its face. On a stone-grey background, the rose-red letters read:

Tomb-Touch Obituary Service

Approve Your Own Obituaries During Your Lifetime. Do Not Risk Unimaginative Obituaries When You Are Not There To Object.

There is now no one to answer your knock, and welcome you in. The board is defaced with tar paint at the lower corners. But still it reads clear. If you peep inside through the window pane, you will find a well-set office. Now it is full of cobwebs and dust. You can make out that it is no longer used.

A young man with greying hair used to sit across a large table holding a pile of files and an old typewriter. Next to him sat his Spanish girl-friend, who spoke a smattering of English. The light skinned man is, because he is still alive, of Indo-French descent. Pompidoux looks like a poet, serious sometimes. He is actually a failed poet. He has invented the profitable profession of *obituarers*, and is now a rich man.

It is an interesting story, how he became an *obituarer*, a word and profession coined by him. The word *obituarer* has still to find a place in any reputed dictionary of the English language. While in the eighth grade, the Mother Superior of his School, Cecil, died. About fifty students wrote her obituary in a spirit of fierce competition. Out of those fifty, two were selected for publication in the school journal; Pompidoux's ranked first. The stern and stony matriarch appeared too waxy in the tale he wrote. The hagiography of the nun was read at the school assembly, the children wept to hear of the nun's virtues. They had never experienced her kindness while she was alive.

Pompidoux learnt a great secret about himself. He was a born *obituarer*! He confirmed his skill by writing more obituaries, including those of the living luminaries. His father laughed at his original pieces and encouraged him. When ninety-year-old Pappadorai, a celebrity of Pondicherry, fell ill and was admitted to the Intensive Care Unit of the General Hospital, Pompidoux wrote a moving obituary, a week in advance. Sooner than Pappadorai's death, Pompidoux's father submitted it to the *Pondicherry Times*. Pompidoux got remuneration and a name in the field.

Gradually his obituaries became a fashion statement for the citizens of Pondicherry. He wrote in French and English, replete with quotes from the Holy Bible, Gita or Thirukural, as was the case. He embellished his writing with his own poetry. Many old people willed it to their children that their obituaries must be written by Pompidoux, and should appear in the prestigious

Pondicherry Times after they were gone.

He used to charge the Tamilians five-thousand rupees and the Europeans ten, for writing excellent obituaries. From the living, who were interested in securing their obituaries in advance to avoid the suspense later, he charged three times or more, depending on the quality of his art work and the pockets of his clients. These days, one could never be certain about what might spring up when a man is no more. Poor language skills, and lack of original ideas in the *obituarers*, are at the root of this anxiety in a would-be-dead.

One can still read the blow-ups of newspaper clippings on the walls of his deserted office. A few quotes are reproduced here:

'Like a butterfly from its chrysalis, an angel has hatched out of Mr. XXX.'

'Soul incubates in body like a peacock in the egg. To the merriment of the seraphs, a cherub is born (out of Mr. XZ).'

'The flood of tears could not wash her memories from the rock of time.'

'Constructing biographies is as formidable as describing the form of an iceberg. How can one judge and profile a man who surpasses his physical and vital moulds, the only tangible entities in him?'

'He was a mountain peak that dazzles in the last rays of the setting sun.'

'The matriarch in her matched the Mother Earth.'

'May he live in bliss in his afterlife (in his grave).' Or, 'May the fairies delight him there.'

He always painted a grave as a bed of roses, an annexe of Paradise on earth. He never gave a thought to the novel bed-fellows, toads and spiders.

So on and so forth, he produced most astonishing obituaries. The eyes of his would-be clients, mostly rich and old folk, would moisten with joy, hearing their obituary sung while still kicking in their bodies. His obituaries spoke well of the taste and class of the dead. Each quality of a client acquired a divine grandeur. He even invented newer qualities in his clients like 'a never understood sense of humour'. A miser would be moved to learn of his covert charitable nature. He even composed music of his obituary songs, and charged a lakh of rupees. He became a rich man.

His obituaries were a riot of fancy. He was a trend-setter and a pioneer of the new craft hitherto unknown to the people of Pondicherry. Even the jilted adolescent lovers lurked near his studio. By the way, Pondicherry has the highest suicide rate in the country as of now (2005).

He pioneered a sort of mass hysteria amongst the people, paralleled only by the pop stars. Instead of gold or M.F. Husain, people in the town preferred to buy obituaries as a sort of investment in future. It was a solid saving. The rates increased rapidly every year.

A crop of *obituarers* followed, but none was as creative as our Pompidoux. The likes of 'Paradise *Obituarers*' and 'Heaven Graves', were mere poor fakes.

Pompidoux successfully created the sort of need in the citizens of Pondicherry. His obituaries became part of the death ceremony of the Hindus and Christians. The fire spread to other towns as well. Tamilians are emotional people. For a cinema actor or a political cause they can go to any extent, including committing suicide. Such calamities filled his coffers. The political parties would pay him over his normal rate for writing a rabble-rousing obituary for their leaders to read at such funerals.

In the heat of the municipal corporation election, he sold himself to a political party. He wrote funny obituaries for the opponents. The creative obituaries actually made the opponents a household name. People remembered the opponents only for the songs on them. The opposition won by a thumping majority. The obituaries he wrote for the opponents were worth over lakhs of rupees. The goons of the party he supported, vandalised his shop, and damaged his board. They set the shops of other *obituarers* on fire.

Pompidoux had made a serious error of judgment. He realised his mistake. It was time for him to spread out. He moved to Chennai, a three hour-drive from Pondicherry.

The loss to Pondicherry was a gain to Chennai. Pompidoux now heads the obituary division of a leading newspaper in Chennai. He has elevated the obituary section in the newspaper to the level of supplements on finance and sport, the section surpasses the pages on local events. The obituary is now a well established literary art form in India. It is included as a special paper on the course on Journalism in the local university at Pondicherry.

He still freelances. For a short piece he charges rupees fifty thousand. A very moving song may cost a lakh or more, for a music composition there is a negotiable charge.

□

The Food Pot

My grandma is a rustic woman from the backwoods of Bulandshahar. She has now become very old and sick and has completely lost control over herself. She passes water without knowing about it. Her slovenly appearance always annoys my parents.

My mother and father have shifted her out of our house that my grandpa had built, to another relative in Shakurbasti. Her locality is not as clean and good as ours. However, everything is cheaper there, the neighbours are kind and helpful, says my grandma. There, the poor people can manage their lives better than anywhere else in Delhi. My grandmother now lives happily with her widowed niece who resembles her.

I love my grandmother. She tells such interesting tales. I have beautiful memories of the time she lived with us. Each evening, despite my mother's scolding, I used to go to her dark and dingy room, hide in her piss-smelling quilt, and pester her for stories. I hated her quilt but I liked her body odour. It put me to sleep before she could finish her story. She is never tired of telling me stories.

When I was a baby, my mother used to leave for work. In the hot afternoons I would go to my grandma. Her electric fan seldom worked. She fanned me with a palm-leaf hand-fan till I fell asleep. When my mother returned, I would rush to her pretendi ıg relief from my grandma's company. That would please my mother.

Nowadays Grandma comes with her niece, they stay in her old room for the day, and return in the evening. She comes wearing a diaper to avoid discomfort to my parents. I know that she comes only to see me, for no one else is bothered about her. But no one else knows this fact. I quietly go to her room and eat the sweets she brings. I know that the sweets are not good and clean, but I eat them to make her happy. I do not let my parents know about this, for they would object to my consuming filth.

Recently, I have observed that her hands have started shaking. She has become very unsteady. She often collides with objects in the room and on the street, and trips. I fear that she may fall from the bus and die one day. We would not even know about it.

We had a special pot at home in which she was served her meals. I have told you already that her hands shake, and she spills things. She cannot handle her spoon now. I put a newspaper under her pot so that she may eat in comfort without the fear of spilling anything on the floor.

Last Saturday, my grandma visited us. She was served her meal in the same pot. She put water in her pot to drink. Suddenly, her hands shook and the pot tumbled down making a noise. I immediately cleaned the place so that no one could notice the pieces of the pot.

My mother has something called the sixth sense; she comes to know of everything that I secretly attempt. No one can hide any wrong or misdoings from her eyes. She rushed out of her kitchen and said that she knew that the old woman had broken the pot, and I had hidden the pieces. She became very angry with grandma's clumsiness and my untruthfulness.

I too felt very upset with my grandma, this time. I chided her for being always clumsy and careless. I asked her, 'Now where would I serve food to my own mother in her old age?'

My mother called me a serpent up the sleeve, and wept at my ill-conceived speech. It was a mistake on my part. I will never use such a pot for my parents. Parents deserve the best in their twilight years for what they do for us in their youth.

□

Buddha

The valley of Lahaul Spiti in the north of India, borders Tibet. There is a small town in the valley. It has only one road which runs in tight and parallel spirals over the hill. All the houses and shops are located along it. The town has beautiful Gompas (Buddhist temples) and is full of lamas and student monks. It is famous for its yak wool, carpets, religious embroidery and paintings, and artwork on metal and wood. In the winter months, blizzards and avalanches from the mountains block all the passes and roads to the valley. In the rainy season unpredictable landslides on the way make the area dangerous. Access to the town was very difficult in the earlier days. Now, cars and trucks can reach here. In summer, the town looks resplendent and colourful. Tourists come here.

The Indian army has made a base here. It remains stationed throughout the year for the fear of Chinese occupation.

It was an early winter morning, cold and chilly. The valley lay covered under fresh snow. It blazed blue under the moonlight. The sun was still to rise. The nocturnal creatures, foxes, wolves, panthers, deer, flying squirrels and bats withdrew into their hideouts in anticipation. The people in the town were still asleep. However the monasteries had woken up and were humming the chant of *Om Mani Padme Hum*.

That morning, the early birds saw a curious spectacle. Lama

Geshe was running through the narrow lanes, jogging down and striding uphill through the serpentine u-turns. Although he had covered his face, his height, contour and gait made one certain that it was him. He would walk a distance and then look back to see if someone was following him. He would appear and disappear through the snow-white lanes like a maroon fish diving deep and surfing up over the milky waves. He appeared to be anxious. Following the path walked by him, a well clad woman in blue jeans appeared and disappeared on his trail.

The monk stopped in front of a monastery and looked back. The woman was still there. She was breathless and walking up with difficulty. He quickly bowed and entered a small hole in a huge wooden gate, guarding the entrance of a monastery, and disappeared inside. The woman reached there and shouted, 'Hanif'. The guard pulled the shutter on her face. The disappointed woman wiped her tears and slowly backtracked through the same curvatures, climbs and declines.

Hanif was a bright boy enrolled in the English-honours course at Delhi University. His parents had immigrated to India from Bamiyan, a small town in Afghanistan. The town had beautiful statues of Buddha on the cliffs of the Hindukush. These serene statues fascinated him as a child. His father had told him that Buddha was an Indian prophet. The people called the Prophet, Baba.

He was fascinated by Baba. He used to see the Prophet in his dreams and imagination The Prophet effusing the light of a thousand suns would come to him and play in a surreal field. Hanif would kneel and pray at his feet. He often saved the best pieces of beef to feed the Prophet. He collected beautiful poppy flowers, and offered those to Buddha. The Prophet smiled at him. Little Hanif saw him through the eyes of his mind. His heart always cried out to the Prophet for everything and anything. He would speak of his hopes and disappointments to the Prophet and feel content at His benign and protective smile. He would recite *namaz* to him and feel happy. On holidays the family would wander in the caves of the mountain where a thousand Buddhist monks lived. Long ago, they were slain by the zealots.

Flocks of tourists used to come to Bamiyan from all corners of the world. They were so fascinated by the statues that they did not mind commuting thousands of miles in all kinds of conveyances. They told Hanif more and more about the Prophet who lived twenty-five hundred years ago.

He felt proud of his town, the home of a thousand devotees of the Prophet. Were the *Hazaras*, meaning the thousand ones in Persian, the children of Buddha? He often wondered. He felt the Prophet as his own great grandfather and protective angel.

Every day, the Taliban grew in strength. They spread over the villages and towns. They took over the administration of the country. They arrived in the valley of Bamiyan as well. Freedom lover *Hazaras* fought like lions but lost to them.

The Taliban considered the Shiite *Hazaras* of Bamiyan as kafirs and monitored madarsas. They roamed at nights and peeped into the houses. They banned music and laughter. Many happy people were murdered, for their irrepressible happiness. Simple pleasures of life, and modern education were un-Islamic, they said. Everything modern and everything ancient in the valley of *Hazaras*, be it a beautiful rose or pretty smile of a little girl, or the beautiful figures of Baba, were considered evil and against the religion of Taliban. *Hazara* women were denied fresh air. They were ordered to wrap themselves in layers of gauze to save the men folk from lust. The black veil was imposed on the colourful costumes of pink *Hazara* women. Love was declared a heinous crime.

His father had no alternative but to withdraw his sisters from the school. The family could not hear or sing music for fear of the mullahs. His sister's childhood sweetheart was beheaded by some spiritual figure. Tourists to Bamiyan took to their heels. The business of *Hazara* people declined. Hanif's family restaurant closed down.

Under Taliban shelling when many homes burnt, and *Hazaras* killed, his heart called out to Baba for the protection of his own family. Baba, he felt, drew a wall of silence around his house. In the morning when people wailed, the neighbouring house was punctured with shell fire, all was safe in his house. They thanked Allah.

One day, the family packed up their essentials in small back-sacks and quietly left Bamiyan to attend the wedding of a relative in Peshawar in Pakistan. From Peshawar they went to Lahore and from there to Dubai, and then they arrived in Delhi. Delhi was full of *Hazaras*. Here they found many of their relatives and tribesmen.

They lived in a mosque for some time. Soon they found a house in Lajpat Nagar and moved to it. They opened a roadside dhaba and prepared Afghani nans (bread) and kababs. Hanif got admission to the Jamia Millia School and passed with flying colours. He was admitted to the prestigious Sri Venkateshwara College of Delhi University.

Baba was still in his heart.

Sundari was the most beautiful girl of the college and was in her second year. As was the custom of the college, she ragged the newcomer with great enthusiasm. 'What is your name, Chinky?' she asked Hanif.

'Hanif,' he answered coyly.

She was amazed to hear his name, 'But you look Buddhist, a man from Dalai Lama's Kingdom.'

'I am a Moslem Buddhist from Bamiyan. We have the biggest statues of Buddha in our town.'

'Moslem Buddhist! Never heard of such a thing! Sounds like *Bakri Singh*!'

'I haven't understood,' Hanif said in a low tone.

Sundari helpfully added, 'Tube light! Haven't you ever seen a chimera?'

Hanif kept quiet.

'Chimera is a hybrid, Chinky. Haven't you seen a chimera of goat and ...?'

Hanif seemed uncertain.

'What is the other animal?' Sundari threatened.

'Sheep!' Hanif quizzed.

'You fool! It is a lion. A goat who is a lion at the same time is *Bakri Singh*,' Sundari explained.

He took some time, but understood, 'Ha ha ha!' He laughed like a child, showing his pearly teeth. 'My ancestors came from Mongolia along with Ghengiz Khan. In Mongolia they became Buddhist. We were Buddhist too but became Moslems. I love Buddha, and keep him in my heart.' The boy said.

They clicked well. Hanif joined Sundari's gang, a group of smart boys and girls. He was nicknamed Buddhu, a fool. The gang sometimes skipped classes and explored the far crannies of Delhi. One day, the gang went to the main campus of Delhi University in the north end of the city, some twenty kilometres far. There they met a boy who looked like Hanif, light skinned and pink with high cheek bones and mongoloid features.

Hanif was pleased. He said, 'Wale-kum-Salaam.' The man did not understand. Hanif repeated his greeting. The boy replied in broken English that he was a Buddhist. Hanif was surprised. He saw an actual Buddhist for the first time. He invited the *Hazara* looking boy for a cup of tea with their gang. The boy accepted their invitation. He was a Buddhist from the Tibetan settlement in *Manjnu-Ka-Tila*. Hanif felt as if he was waiting for Dorje for lives, to hear about Buddha, the prophet of his own town and heart. Dorje, too, was amazed to hear of Buddha in the cliffs of Hindukush in far-off Bamiyan valley. They exchanged contact addresses and parted.

Dorje would often come to the college canteen to see the gang, particularly Hanif. The two had developed a deep bond of friendship. Hanif too would go to Tibet Town to meet his new friend. The area was notorious for drug peddlers, as for its Buddha temples. The gang members noted Hanif's frequent absence from their group.

One day, Hanif came to the college and informed the gang that he would not continue his classes any more. His classmates were very surprised. Hanif was doing well in his studies. Sundari was shocked. She asked, 'But why so, Buddhu?'

He said, 'It is a waste of my time. What use is this education to me?'

'A B.A. is the minimum qualification to get a respectable job.'

'For those, who want a job! I don't want one. I will bake bread, or may be, return to Bamiyan where there is no college and job.'

The gang argued with him but to no avail. After all he was a Buddhu! He would come irregularly and sit in the canteen, and wait for Dorje. The two would take a ride off to the Tibet Town.

His father came one day to meet the principal. He looked very anxious. Hanif had not come home for the past two days. He met Hanif's friends to locate his whereabouts. Sundari told him about Hanif's new friend, Dorje in the Tibet Town. Eventually his father found him in Tibet Town, and brought him back.

Sundari felt very anxious for her friend. Such episodes had become common. Hanif reappeared, continued for several days and then suddenly disappeared. But each time he came, he appeared cheerful and cool. He never appeared like a boy who ran away from home without informing his family, and skip classes for no reason. He was a good boy, and now appeared better.

It was March, the month of their examination, in 2001. Hanif was not seen for several days. One day, he suddenly reappeared on the way to the canteen. He asked Sundari out to the canteen. He looked very disturbed. That day, Sundari suspected that he had fallen in love with her. It seemed to her that for her only, Hanif had come to the college. While walking towards the canteen with Hanif, she kept guessing the reason behind his strange behaviour. His face contorted, he took a few short breaths as if he was about to sob. She felt dismayed. She held out her hands, and held his hands to reassure him of her support. He said nothing and became calm.

Further down the path, Hanif suddenly turned and wept like a little imp. Sundari wiped his tears with her *dupatta*. She drew him to her breast like a mother and consoled, 'No, Buddhu, No! Don't cry. Everything will be all right. Let me know what has happened.'

'They have fired at my heart. They have torn me apart. Talibans have destroyed my Baba in Bamiyan.' He sobbed and cried loudly, 'Who will take flowers from me now? Whom will I offer my meals? With whom will I share my heart, to whom will I offer my prayer? About a hundred *Hazaras* were also killed by them, including my father's brother.'

'Do not cry on account of mad people. Can anyone kill Buddha? It was only the stone engraving. Do not grieve. I see Buddha alive in your heart. He is there at his rightful place. He will never abandon you.' Sundari lifted his chin up and reassured him, 'Smile now.'

Buddhu wiped his tears and smiled.

Soon after, Hanif was not seen. Sundari missed him the most in her gang. She went often to Hanif's house in Lajpat Nagar to inquire about him, but no one seemed to know of his whereabouts. His mother wailed for her son. Even Dorje did not have any idea. The police, friends and relatives, all of them together, searched for him everywhere, but he could not be located anywhere. They wrote him off.

The gang members passed out, and parted. They went their own ways. Some found jobs, others enrolled themselves for a Master's course; a few girls married. Though the friends retained their old bonds, new workplaces brought in newer friends and alignments.

Sundari had married a young army officer, now posted at the valley of Lahaul Spiti. The husband and wife lived in the family barracks. She often remembered and missed the remarkable *Hazara* boy; she wondered where the boy had disappeared.

This was a very small town; it had a few restaurants and not a single cinema hall. There were not many places for the families to go for recreation and fun. The couple spent their evenings visiting the Gompas, each famous for one thing or another. They admired the ancient artwork, rotated the prayer wheel, and made offerings to Buddha. Sundari was fascinated by Buddha. Buddha reminded her of Buddhu. They would sometimes drink *chang*, the Tibetan beer and come back. Time passed.

On the eve of that eventful day, the main Gompa of the town had a special prayer dance to celebrate the rebirth of a high Lama. Lamas congregated in the town from the distant mountains and valleys. Some of them had smuggled themselves out of Tibet through secret passes to witness the incarnation. The town wore festive flags all over the buildings, and looked bright and colourful. The couple had come to the main Gompa to watch the colourful dance of the masked monks to the tune of huge blow-horns, drums, and cymbals.

After sunset, when the dance of the monks was over, a crowd of the local people, lamas, and army men thronged to the altar to pay obeisance to Buddha. They offered silken scarves, lit incense sticks and candles at the altar, bowed and prayed till pushed away by the impatient crowd. A monk stood there in front of the altar. He blessed each visitor by touching his head with a peacock feather and chanting *Om Mani Padme Hum*. The couple jostled to find their way to the altar; they lit a candle and bowed to Buddha and the monk. The monk placed the feather on Sundari's head and chanted the blessings to the bowed woman. The surging queue pushed the couple away.

The monk's veiled face reminded Sundari of someone. Her face was lit with a warm smile. She turned back and shouted gaily, 'Buddhu!' The huge restless crowd jostled and pushed from behind. Sundari turned back again, the monk with the veil was gone. Another unmasked monk with a serene face now chanted in his place. Sundari was trapped in the crowd which moved and pushed in all directions. Her husband lent her a helping hand and pulled her out.

The next morning, when the town was fast asleep, Sundari had come out again to look for someone in the Gompa.

'Where have you been so early, darling?' her husband asked. Clutching the hot mug tightly to her breast, Sundari confessed, 'I found and lost Hanif again.'

'........,'...

'...,'...

'But I would never be lost to you, my darling. Trust me,' her husband reassured her with a charming smile.

□

The Shepherd and the Wolf

There was a temple on the top of a mountain. A priest lived in it. He was a crazy man. He delighted in scaring people and made them believe that he had miraculous and dreadful powers. The frightened faces pleased him.

In the yard, on the east side of the temple, there was a cedar tree. The tree produced a solid shadow against the temple light at night. Further east, down the slope, towered a gigantic oak tree; it camouflaged the moon. Its dense and crooked branches absorbed the moonlight. The slender moonbeams, on the black shadow of the cedar, appeared like white clouds stitched to the ground. When the oak swayed on windy nights, the silvery spots throbbed and gyrated.

Sometimes the priest cast his own mottled shadow against the temple light on moonlit nights, and frighten the curious visitors. Other times, he would make dreadful suggestions about those fluorescent spots on his silhouette to the ears of the petrified villagers. He looked spooky on such nights.

He had also spread the rumour that he used to become a werewolf at night. People believed him, and were duly afraid of him. They would run away and hide from his sight at night. Even the bravest man of the village chickened out at his sight. That pleased him no end.

He had a young friend, a shepherd, who too liked to frighten the villagers. The two men devised ingenious methods to frighten people with their antics. They would roar with laughter behind their backs. They were quite satisfied with their successes.

The shepherd had a new idea. He would go to the hill with his sheep. After a while he would shout aloud, 'Help, help! Save me. A wolf has come.' The villagers would go running armed with their sticks and sickles, and return tricked. The shepherd then laughed at them. This happened a number of times.

One night, the shepherd lay near the temple. A real wolf arrived. He was very hungry. Looking at the shepherd lying all alone, the wolf's mouth watered. Before the shepherd could run the beast sprang on his neck. The shepherd cried loudest, 'Help, help, wolf, wolf!' This time the villagers ignored his call.

The priest heard him and ran in panic to save his friend. The shepherd was unconscious by now. The priest saw a real wolf settled on his friend's chest and chewing his neck. The wolf looked angrily at the priest and snarled at him menacingly. The priest withdrew a little. The wolf stared again at the priest, and found him plump and juicy. The wolf now changed his mind in favour of the priest. The priest understood the wolf's evil intention. He ran back. The wolf chased after him. The priest galloped inside the temple and bolted the door on the face of the blood-dripping animal. The animal walked round the place to find an entry inside, and then walked away disappointed to its dead prey. The commotion on the hill top petered out.

Next morning, the shepherd was discovered dead in the vicinity of the temple. His body bore the wolf's teeth marks. He was partly eaten up. The villagers were horrified to see the blood stains and footprints of the wolf in the direction of the temple. Men were really scared now. Now there was no doubt left as to what had happened to the shepherd.

The men went home, organised themselves with batons, crowbars and axes. They gathered courage and returned. They dragged the priest out from the temple. The priest repeatedly swore that he was no werewolf, he had just joked with them. 'It was a real wolf who attacked the shepherd.' He begged their pardon for scaring them all those days. He pleaded with them to spare his life. They did not believe him this time. Notwithstanding the priest's oath and appeals they hacked the werewolf to death. The two friends unhappily joined each other in hell.

□

The Washerwoman

Piari means a darling, a sweetheart. She was a charming woman with golden skin and black hair. She was a clever talker and a coquette. She was in her mid-twenties. Many young men eyed her. She raised their hopes but never fulfilled them. Piari was a jovial washerwoman. She would go from house-to-house to distribute and collect clothes. She would never keep her word and was never on time despite a thousand promises. The irritated housewives swore to dismiss her but her fantastic excuses seven days a week and pledges overpowered them. In fact the housewives only threatened; they never meant to throw her out, for she enlightened them vividly on what went on in other houses and her own. She was an entertainer of sorts.

She quarrelled with her husband and also her mother-in-law. She was unable to tolerate fat Kamala who always tried to throw her weight on her irrepressible daughter-in-law. Both suspected each other's morals. During their creative quarrels, they invented salacious stories against each other for public consumption. Sometimes, her father-in-law and her husband had to beat their respective spouses to stop them from washing their dirty linen in public. Piari openly challenged her husband that he was not his father's son. Had he really been one, he would have thrown his mother out of their house. The mother-in-law too regretted having fed her milk to a son who watched his mother being insulted by a slut. She would wail and ask for rat poison to end her life.

On other occasions, the two women would make up and appear as the best of friends, and walk hand-in-hand distributing and collecting clothes. They would allow each other laughter and fun with their clients and beaus. They were always well-dressed. They had no qualms about wearing clients' good saris before returning, or even pilfering them. While returning home with sacks of clothes, they would amuse the vegetable vendors with their coquettish chatter, bargain and fleece them.

Like unexpected clouds in the summer sky, their quarrels broke out over any matter, cooking or other chores. One day Piari felt that she could no longer live with her husband's mother. She sweetly asked Mithai Lal, her husband, to rent another house and live separately from his parents.

'But our income is not sufficient. All the houses are my mother's clients.'

'Don't you worry dear, I will split them in my favour. The *sethani*[1] always says that your mother-in-law returns dirty clothes, perhaps without washing, and overcharges her. She always calls her names. I am certain they and many other unhappy clients will shift to us.'

'Shut up you slut. You always plot against my mother. You want to break-up our heaven-like home.'

'Heaven-like? Bah! Good heavens!' She snorted contemptuously. 'I am being roasted alive in the worst of hells. You call it a heaven. That whore is jealous of my beauty. What can I do if God has made her so ugly and vicious,' she retorted.

'How dare you call my mother an ugly whore? You, swine!' The son slapped Piari on both her cheeks.

Proud of her son, the mother-in-law arrived on the scene like a gust of wind. 'I was mad to have brought you to my house. The whole town knows that you were born fourteen months after the death of your *baap*[2]. Your real *baap*, the bastard *Baid*[3], certified that children could even be born after two years of pregnancy.'

'As if father-in-law is Mithai's *baap*. That son of a bitch, Kallan, your paramour begot him. Your own mother-in-law declared that in the hearing of the whole town. Peace be upon her! The impotent bastard now stares at me.'

The mother-in-law screamed at her, 'Hold your tongue, bitch.'

'You call me a bitch? May your tongue rot, and worms devour it,' Piari retorted.

Mithai slapped Piari again and disappeared.

Piari decided enough is enough, and she must do something to end all this. She did not sleep the whole night. She tossed in bed drawing up one scheme after another. Next morning, she did not wake Kamala; served her tea right in bed. She pressed Kamala's legs like a dutiful daughter-in-law and told Kamala that the latter deserved some rest in life. Kamala was pleased at Piari's sudden change of heart. She was tempted to take a little more advantage. She said, 'My Piari, I am not feeling well today. Can I rest for the whole day? Today you look after the clients,' she lay down again in bed.

'You must rest mother-in-law. You have grown old and must look after your health. I will go to the clients today on my own. Tomorrow, only if you feel better, you may join me. You are my mother as well,' Piari said sweetly like a new bride.

Piari dressed to kill. She looked very charming. She collected her baggage and set out. Kamala did not like her going out so well dressed and made-up. She said to herself, 'Sure, she has tricked me today; must be going to meet her boys.' But the idea of complete rest pleased her and she decided not to investigate the matter any further.

Piari knocked at Pappu's door. Fortunately Pappu, and not his mother, opened the door. He leered at her and grinned broadly. He whispered, 'So early, my sweetheart. Where are you going?'

She threw the clothes bundle at him and said in an undertone, 'I will come to your shop at twelve. Will you be there?'

'By all means, Piari.'

Piari reached Gandhi Provision Store in time. She addressed Pappu flirtatiously and asked for a sachet of rat poison in jaggery. Pappu gave her two sachets and did not accept the payment. She went away happily. Thinking of her, Pappu kept whistling for long.

Kamala had decided to take full advantage of Piari's generosity. When Piari arrived home, Kamala was still in bed. Piari was annoyed that she had now to cook the meal as well. But she suppressed her feeling. After all Kamala was at her last gasp. She must give her a pleasant farewell, she thought. She set out cooking. She did it really fast, and by the time her husband and father-in-law returned, the meal was ready. All ate well. Kamala was still in bed, malingering. Piari took a *thali*[4], laden with victuals, to Kamala. Kamala ate reclining on her bed. She enjoyed the food, washed her hands in the *thali*, gargled and spat in the empty soup bowl, burped with satisfaction, and lay down again. Piari sat rubbing a balm on Kamala's head.

After a while Piari felt disappointed, nothing was happening to Kamala. The mother-in-law enjoyed all the attention and service. Piari felt like throttling the *witch* who could even digest rat poison with such ease. She cursed the wily Pappu in her heart. 'Men are faithless,' she ruminated.

In the evening when nothing happened, Piari regained her own nature and taunted Kamala for malingering and troubling her. They again fought a battle, neighbours in the guise of well-wishers assembled to enjoy the spectacle. The scene ended with a violent intervention by the men of the house.

At night, Kamala experienced unquenchable thirst and a terrible stomach ache. *Baidji*, whom Kamala used to abuse behind his back, came and advised her to be moved to the hospital. The two men pedalled Kamala to a hospital on a hammock tied between their cycles. Kamala bled from her nostrils. She was put on an intravenous drip. She needed blood for transfusion. Blood group

'B negative' was not available at the hospital. Mithai Lal came back home, collected some neighbours and Piari for blood matching and donation.

As often in such situations, it was Piari's blood that matched, and Piari had no choice but to offer her blood. She in fact forgot her animosity for Kamala, and now realised that she loved her and wanted her to live. The young doctor on duty was the son of her client. She confessed the truth to the doctor, and wept touching his feet to save her mother-in-law. She offered her gold bangles to the doctor. The doctor told her to remain silent about it or it would become a police case.

Two days later, Kamala opened her eyes, and found Piari folding her soiled bed sheet. Piari was so delighted to see Kamala awake that she rushed to embrace her. Kamala drew her close in happiness. Kamala was discharged and they went home happily.

Gradually, the new found love vanished, and their heart-burn returned. Bitter battles ensued. The men beat the women to silence. Piari wept at her foolishness of saving Kamala. Kamala too forgot all about Piari's gift of life. She prayed that plague together with cholera befall her barren daughter-in-law. She clandestinely negotiated another marriage for her son.

One day, Kamala again did not step out of her room. Piari abused the old hag and her antics. When the men went away, she barged into her room calling her names. Kamala did not turn or move. She remained quiet. She was lying on the edge of the bed with her back facing Piari. Piari feared something untoward this time. Retaining her poise, she asked harshly, 'What is the matter? Why don't you get up? Want to enjoy the day at my expense? I curse the day I saved you.'

Kamala did not respond. Piari became curious. She went near her and shook her hard. Kamala fell on the ground like a bolster. Piari found that her eyes were open, and she was not breathing. Surely, she was dead. Piari let off a piercing scream. The neighbours rushed in. One went to call Mithai and his father.

Piari beat her chest and wailed in the customary sing song manner (peculiar to that culture), '*Hai hai*, why did you leave me Amma, with whom will I fight now? Pardon me this time and open your eyes. *Hai hai*.' Piari never thought that Kamala would actually die. She wept, and truly missed her mother-in-law that day.

---

1. Sethani is the address for a seth's (a rich man) wife.
2. *Baap* is a derogatory term for sire in Hindi.
3. *Baid* is an indigenous practitioner of alternative medicine.
4. A metallic food plate.

Two Men and a Dream

Strangely, two friends who spent a night in an underground vault, shared a frightening dream. They confirmed from each other that they saw the same dream, experienced the same figures, colours, odours, sounds and space. Very strange!

It happened over a century ago in a small lake town of the Himalayas. Those days, Nainital was populated by British civilian officers, army men and retired people, apart from the Anglo-Indians, local Christians and the natives. The place reminded the British of their own highlands. They had renamed the mountains of the Himalayas after the mountains back home.

The turquoise blue waters of the Lake Naini are set tightly midst the reclining feet of the surrounding mountains. From the hill tops it appears like a gazelle's blue eye. Its southern border swills over the root of a steep hill which culminates in Ben Nevis (now Van Nivas of Sri Aurobindo Ashram). And, the northern shore is a one and a half mile long strip of flat land. A cobbled street, now no more there, ran through through the flat land, alongside the lake. The flat land gradually rises up into a mountain.

Those days, there were beautiful marts, churches, clubs, restaurants and hotels along the street. At night, dim lights from these buildings glimmered in the still waters of the lake, creating a mirror image of the street. It appeared as if a mysterious town pulsated in the lake at night.

Behind the buildings on the Mall Road, as the street was called, was a slanting area, inhabited by the Europeans. The Eurasian quarters were at a further elevation. Indian Christians settled between the hill folk and the Eurasians. It was a hierarchy of sorts. The Indians were neither welcomed in the lakeside settlement, nor were they strictly forbidden by any official decree. Sometimes, hill folk did come down to enjoy the lake view in the evenings, and visit the temple of Naina Devi through the English quarters. Particularly, the young boys enjoyed watching and wooing the fair maidens of Europe, and of mixed races at the Mall Road.

One evening, two young Indian converts, Summer Singh and Gaje Simon decided to come down and drink whisky in a lakeside bar, and of course to ogle at the fair and fashionable girls. They had their dinner at Hotel Stockton and walked to the Irish Tavern. It was a cold night, it had snowed that day. The heating in the bar made people warm and comfortable. The two ordered full pegs of whisky. They lost count after a few rounds, and could only remember the last two pegs they drank. Therefore, they continued.

It was eleven at night; the two Eurasian bar girls, Irene and Leena, packed up to move out. They were sisters. A horse carriage waited for them outside. They smiled at the boys on a drinking binge. Gaje could not believe his eyes at the smile of Lady Luck that night. Summer smiled back.

The girls returned to their table. Gaje invited them for a cup of coffee. The two girls joined them, not for coffee, but for a glass of sherry. The boys were delighted. It was a windfall. They never hoped for that. One or two drunkards were still in the bar. The church tower chimed twelve strokes, it was midnight. The barman brought the bill expecting them to leave.

The four were pushed on a horse carriage standing outside the bar, by the disgusted barmen. The driver prodded his horse to action, and the carriage moved up westwards. All were half asleep. It was a moonlit night. The snow sheet shone like a silver-spread over the valley and mountainside. The carriage moved through moonlit fields, small hamlets and pitch dark jungles. At night, the eyes of wild animals glinted in the light of the carriage. Foxes loomed larger than a real tiger. They now passed through the pitch dark oak woods; the girls were frightened; they had clung to the boys' shoulders.

Suddenly the horse stopped. It neighed and raised its forelegs, as if it saw some danger. Two men, well covered in overcoats, and each mounted on a horse, appeared at either side of the coach. They pulled open the doors of the carriage. They peeped in, and the older man spoke harshly, 'Don't you know the time, dear? It is two o'clock. Your mother is still awake and worrying about you. Isn't it shameful?' The boys and girls jumped out of the carriage in confusion.

A flying squirrel flew across Summer's face, chilling his spine. An animal shrieked, perhaps a wolf pounced on it. The father said, 'No, no, sit inside. It is chilly outside. Let's reach home fast.' The girls climbed back into the carriage. The frightened boys kept out. The father thought for a moment, and then he poked Gaje with his whip, 'Wish to die? Get inside, it is too cold.'

A wave of fear passed through the bones of the boys. They shivered. The doors were fastened by the coachman. The coachman patted his horse, and the wheels rolled again. The coach reached an open field. Hares and deer wallowed over the snow in the moonlight. The horse slowed down and negotiated a dangerous climb. They could hear the three men talking in pidgin English. Their voices appeared to come from a distance, nothing was discernible. They realised that they were drunk.

In an hour, all of them reached a dark foyer with a huge door. The coachman, father of the girls and her brother forced open the door. It creaked and opened with difficulty. The girls alighted and entered with the men.

The coachman returned from inside to take the boys to their

respective homes. The father followed him; he requested them to stay there for the night as a snowstorm was brewing in the sky. They could return in the morning. The horseman immediately agreed and untied his horse. He disappeared across the door.

The two terrified boys came out of the carriage and looked at the father uncertainly. The father now appeared warm and kind. He asked them to follow him. He took them down through a short flight of stairs inside a pitch dark chamber. He, familiar with the place, walked straight to the grate and lit it; bid them a warm goodnight and left them with a bottle of brandy.

In the dim light of yellow flames, they explored the room. There was no bed in the room. It had only a carpet, a few cushioned sofa chairs and long rectangular wooden boxes. There were some candles over the boxes. They had nothing to cover themselves with. They decided to sit near the fireplace and spend the night. Soon, they fell asleep.

It was a terrible storm outside. One could hear the noise of shaking trees and the wind battering everything on its way. It was a horrible night. They heard a knock on the door.

The two girls slid out of their beds. They pushed the door, and entered; they latched the door from inside and smiled at the boys. The flames grew taller and the room was well lit now. The girls looked angelic. They had brought coffee and edibles. The boys were ravenous and they finished the food and coffee. They did not leave one morsel of food for the girls. The girls smiled and asked them if they wanted more.

Someone banged on the door. The sound became louder with each bang. The father asked them to open the door. The frightened girls leapt out of the window. The boys felt dizzy when they looked out of the window, for it was only a cliff on the mountain top. Down, two thousand feet below the steep cliff, a silvery river flowed. Any fall would have battered their bones and flesh to pieces. Wolves howled below. Fortunately there were steel holdfasts all over the wall. The girls assured them of their safety and moved down over the wall like trapeze artists. The boys were horrified. It was the most adventurous night of their lives. They never felt so terrified.

The door banged and opened, the father and the brother barged in asking for Irene and Leena. Gaje held his breath, and lied that no one had come there. The father was not convinced. He looked at the open window. He went to the window and looked down. There was nothing. He begged their pardon, and went back hailing 'Irene', and the brother shouted, 'Leena'. Their voices echoed. The boys closed the door. The girls wriggled in through the window, and gestured to them to remain silent. The arms of the girls were bruised by the frozen stone wall. Their fine clothes were torn and grimy now. The boys heaved a sigh of relief. It had grown chilly inside. The boys opened the bottle and sipped brandy, they lit cigarettes and smoked. The girls refused to share their pleasure.

The blizzard was becoming noisier. The wolves had come closer and howled right in their ears. They felt that the wolves were climbing the wall outside the window. Realising their fear, Leena closed the window. The bottle of brandy was nearly over, the candle light had extinguished; the flames were dying. They felt very drowsy. All the four spread over the carpet, and were soon snoring.

A cock crowed somewhere. Summer used to wake up at the first cock crow. He woke up in the dark, the room was still dark. He tried to look for the window. He could not find it. He tumbled over a large wooden box. He came back to wake Gaje. Gaje was fast asleep, he did not move. Summer also lay down and was asleep again.

After a few hours, he heard noises outside. He could hear the hill women passing that way. They were singing to ward off the cold. Summer strained his eyes, it was still pitch dark. He looked for the door, he could not discover it. Like a blind man he thumped his palm and stamped his feet all over, he could not feel the grate, or the fireplace. He stumbled over wooden boxes repeatedly. After a while he saw a dim ray of light through a narrow slit. He lay on the ground to look out. He could glimpse little of the outside world. Gaje was also awake by now. The two pushed the door. It did not move. They pushed it harder with all their might, it only creaked.

They heard a frightened voice, 'Lord Jesus Christ!'

They pushed the door harder. 'Who is there?' Someone shouted outside.

Summer replied, 'I am Summer from Isai Bustee. Gaje and I are trapped here. Could you please open the door.'

'How did you get in there?' the voice asked.

'We were drunk and forgot our way last night. I don't know how we have landed here.'

'Are you Manek Masih's son.'

'Yes, yes. Are you Uncle Tony?'

'Yes, my son. Wait, it is latched from outside, I will unfasten the latch.'

They heard the footsteps coming down a staircase. The man opened the latch with great difficulty. It was jammed and covered with cobwebs, as if it was never opened. The man was quite frightened. He pulled the wooden planks with all his might. The door opened. Light came inside. It was an underground vault.

Tony stood outside with a silver cross in his hand and a candle. The boys came out to the familiar world. Inside they noticed six closed wooden boxes. There was no window or a fireplace. Even the cushioned chairs and carpet were not there. Summer and Gaje were surprised, for what they saw at night was not there any more. 'Do you remember the tall girl, Irene?' Summer asked Gaje.

'And Leena as well! There were wolves on the wall,' Gaje replied.

'Yes, I clearly remember that Leena had closed the window,' said Summer.

Both were astonished.

Tony closed the door and fastened the latch. He pulled and pushed the door again to reassure himself. He carefully replaced the cross over the latch. He asked the boys to climb the staircase. Tony followed them and they surfaced on the ground.

There, on the platform over the vault, stood a statue of Virgin Mary. Five names were engraved at her feet in one line—'William and Martha Saunders and their children John, Irene and Leena;' the second line read, 'succumbed to plague in 1869.' It was a shocking experience for them. The boys kept wondering, where Martha was that night. And who was the coachman? Tony had no answers, for he had never experienced the supernatural there. He insisted that there were no such entities as wraiths and ghosts. What the boys saw was a sort of hallucination or some illusion of mind.

'Then how do you explain the names the bar girls told us? I clearly remember it was Irene and Leena,' Summer asked Tony.

'True, the two girls with similar names work in the Irish Tavern. You will find them there now. The horse carriage is owned by the Bar to fetch and drop its employees,' Tony said.

'Then how did we get here? And who locked us in?'

'You would certainly have known, son, had you been a little less drunk. Even now you stink of alcohol,' Tony reprimanded Summer.

'Can two individuals share an identical dream, similar sights, odours and colours?' Summer asked. 'We drank brandy for sure in the vault.'

Gaje blew his breath over the cup of his palm, and smelt it. He said, 'True, we experienced the same incidents. Leena had closed the window to stop the wolves from entering.'

Their jackets still wafted the perfume that the girls wore.

Tony did not believe a single word that the boys told him. He did not want to believe in such nonsense.

□

Monkeys' Religion

Vrindavan, the birthplace of Lord Krishna, near Agra, has a big institute of animal sciences. Prof Radha Binod Das is a scientist in the department of animal psychology. Though, he is famous all over the world, the local people do not like him for what he has done to Vrindavan. He has turned monkeys into bandits here. They rob the pilgrims, beg in the temples and harass children and women. The monkey menace in town is alarming and even policemen are bitten by these scoundrels.

The scourge of the town could be traced back to a Department of Science and Technology (DST) research grant to the professor. The psychology professor made interesting experiments on the effects of reward and punishment on animal behaviour. The experimental set-up was as follows: the laboratory room had a staircase to the roof, where fruit was kept in a concealed bowl. Twelve monkeys were housed in this laboratory. In course of time, all the monkeys discovered the secret location of the fruit bowl. Each of them could climb up, fetch a banana and eat it any time of the day. The arrangement made the monkeys happy.

Once, the monkeys had learnt this skill, the professor modified his experimental design. Now, the fruit-bowl was connected to a touch-sensitive spray shower. Whenever a monkey touched the fruit-bowl, an ice cold shower would drench his companions on the floor. A banana was the reward for a climber; at the same time it became punishment to others. To avoid the ice-cold shower, the monkeys decided among themselves that no one would climb the staircase to fetch a banana.

One hot afternoon, all the monkeys slept after a sumptuous meal. A senior, unable to sleep, quietly got up. He looked around. All his brothers were dozing off. Greed overran his discretion. He slyly observed them for a while. Seemingly, they were lost to the world. He tiptoed on the staircase. To his misfortune, all the others woke up that very moment, and pounded him to the ground before he could actually reach the fruit bowl.

The monkeys had lost patience with their own greed. It was distressing to bathe in ice-cold water now and then, at any ungodly hour. They had decided to beat anyone who climbed the staircase, under any circumstance. The severity of punishment nipped the bud of greed in the monkeys. Thereafter, no one dared to climb the staircase without a risk to his limbs.

Having trained them thus, the professor retired two monkeys of the group. They were released on the street to fend for themselves. The two were now so conditioned that they would neither climb any height nor allow others to do so. They were fanatical about this rule. They thrashed the stray monkeys who attempted to climb a parapet or a tree.

Prof Das replaced the released monkeys with two new monkeys from the wild. Monkeys have a natural curiosity to explore their environment. The fresh recruits explored every nook and cranny of their new surroundings, then they decided to find out where the staircase led. They were ignorant of the law. And, the moment the newcomers stepped on the staircase, they were battered by their seniors. Thus the new ones, who never came to know about the bananas and cold shower, learned to bash any one who tried to climb the staircase. They did not bother to find the rationale behind the exercise. They just followed their seniors enthusiastically.

One-by-one, the remaining monkeys, who knew the reason

for beating the climbers were replaced with new monkeys. The new ones never questioned the utility of the exercise. They seemed to enjoy the ritual. This ritual had become a matter of faith with them. Climbing the staircase was considered shameful and immoral. Beating errant climbers was considered an act of merit, a religious duty. It made them feel pious, happy and joyous. Had someone told them the banana and shower story, they would outright have rejected such a stupid reason as blasphemy.

The study came to an end, scientific conclusions were drawn, and the report was sent to the DST. Prof Das released all the monkeys from captivity.

The monkeys ran to freedom on the streets of Vrindavan. Their conditioning to the novel concept of sin and virtue changed the life of the residents and pilgrims in Vrindavan. These monkeys were self-righteous and ritualistic about the very act of climbing by the other monkeys. These puritans lived and roamed in gangs. They attacked any monkey who attempted to climb a staircase, building or a tree. These were male monkeys, muscular and powerful. Their writ ran on the stray monkeys of Vrindavan. They policed others. Over a period of time, all the rogue monkeys were disciplined by these committed ones.

The dogs of Vrindavan perennially exhibited a vicious hostility towards the monkeys. They used to harass them, chase them and bite them. The monkeys used to climb the trees to escape the dogs. Now the monkeys dared not climb the trees and escape. They feared the new law as much as they feared the dogs. The monkeys who defied the law received a severe retribution by the monkey-police.

The monkeys could no longer enjoy fruit on trees, their staple diet; they starved. They began ruining the tomato and pumpkin crops. The farmers gave them a far severe thrashing. They drew impenetrable fences around their farms. The monkeys could not escape to jungles, for the jungles were not there any more. Since they could not pluck fruit, they stole food from the houses. They became thieves and shoplifters. Beating did not deter them, as non-stealing only meant starvation and death, a punishment far more severe than beating. The citizens of the town closed the openings to their houses, erected walls and put locks on their cabinets and refrigerators. The desperation of the monkeys increased.

Monkeys were the primates before man appeared on our planet. They had engineered novel strategies and devices, essential for their survival. They had developed simple tools. Even now, they show an atavistic reason and pragmatism.

The monkeys took to begging. They turned themselves into pathetic looking beggars. Old and wise monkeys sought alms. They sat amidst the crowd of beggars and monks assembled at the gates of temples. They sat with closed eyes and extended palms like the others. They followed the visitors in line with the other beggars. The pilgrims and worshippers were amused, they acknowledged them as descendants of Lord Hanuman, the monkey god. They were offered good food, soaked gram and *laddoos*. No effort was required by them. The life was just good.

When the number of monkeys proliferated at the temples' gates, the pilgrims were unable to feed all of them. The monkeys fought amongst themselves over the alms.

The puritan monkeys were not concerned with this development. Their only concern was that no one should breach the moral code, that was, to climb a staircase or a tree. Surprisingly, the number of puritanical monkeys also increased. The 'cult of non-climbers' spread like summer fire among the monkeys. Even the female monkeys became religious. They would attack the climbers with religious zeal.

The aggression and violence increased. Animals and men were now petrified of the monkeys. The dogs who chased monkeys, now at their sight sought shelter behind their masters. Monkeys wandered all over Vrindavan like mafiosi.

They scared old women and children. They would pull their saris till they received something from them. They even accepted a coin. They had learnt that the coins could buy them food. They stored the coins. If someone offered them food they happily passed the coins to him. They fought whoever resisted them.

Monkeys identified accomplices amongst men, made friends with them. They adopted a man who helped them in their industry of loot. I will tell you about this symbiotic relationship in the words of Professor Das. 'A monkey would snatch a bag, purse or spectacles of a pilgrim and swiftly disappear. Then, the monkey's agent would arrive on the scene, and console the aggrieved pilgrim and offer his help, of course for some consideration. The agent would demand some money, say five rupees, from the pilgrim. Then he would call the monkey out and place a little food for him at a safe distance. The monkey would then walk from its hideout, collect the food and leave the pilgrim's belongings there. Then the team would walk away to another site, and repeat the operation on another gullible simpleton. Interestingly, many monkeys may share one agent. On the other hand, a super-smart monkey may have several agents. Well, these alliances are dynamic, they keep changing.'

The citizens of Vrindavan complained to the civic authorities and police about the monkey business. The police offered to shoot the monkeys and ease the life of the citizens. However, the *Vaishnava* mayor of the municipal corporation vetoed the suggestion. *Vaishnavas* do not believe in taking life under any provocation; they may lose theirs but not take another's.

The mayor has collected donations from the rich temples and the businessmen of Vrindavan and created a trust to reform the delinquent monkeys. He has written to Prof Radha Binod Das, and offered him funds to begin a new study on this novel symbiosis between animal and man, and find a psychological method to end this. Another proposal, titled, 'The Psychological Basis of Moral and Religious Laws' has been submitted to the Indian Council of Sociological Research by the professor.

□

The Saviour

It was a hot and sultry morning at the Mumbai international airport. It was still dark. The flight from New York had just landed. Hanumant alighted from the aircraft, and walked up to the waiting shuttle-bus. He felt very uneasy. He unbuttoned his collar. He was unable to breathe at the arrival lounge. He sat down and inhaled a puff from his spray. It did not help. He felt that the crowd had consumed all the oxygen in the air. He rushed out to breathe fresh air but found himself choked. He made a tremendous effort to suck in oxygen, but in vain. His driver drove him to the hospital.

Hanumant had developed a persistent cough for the last six months. It had become painful. He swallowed with difficulty, felt short of breath and wheezed all the time. He could not find time to visit his doctor friend; he was too busy in the business of life.

Dr Zhivago examined him and asked for his X-ray. The surgeon looked at the plate against an illuminated box. He pointed ominously to a thistle flower which shone like a star at night. He again examined Hanumant. Hanumant had a tiny nodule in his right arm pit. Zhivago became grim and silent. He did not speak, but Hanumant heard his thought and protested, 'Don't say that doctor. Could it not be something else?'

'Certainly, it could be some benign mass. We will have to

confirm the diagnosis; we will do an MRI to find out the extent and depth of the mass. By clinical examination and simple X ray we cannot determine the size and penetration of an internal growth. Till then please stop smoking, Hanumant. Would you please?' The doctor looked sternly at Hanumant. 'I have been telling you not to smoke for the past several years. You never listened to me.' The doctor rebuked the shocked patient.

Both bronchoscopy and biopsy were performed. The reports confirmed the suspicion. Dr Zhivago informed Hanumant of the diagnosis. It was an adenocarcinoma in the bronchus within the right lung, in simple words—a lung cancer. Hanumant had wished and prayed that the spot be anything but cancer. Listening to the doctor, Hanumant turned pale; his heart throbbed in his throat. He sweated and shivered. He became panicky. He feebly begged, 'I want to live. Don't say that it's incurable. I can go to the US or anywhere you suggest.' Then Hanumant collapsed on the doctor's table. Zhivago helped him to the sofa. Hanumant lay there with his eyes closed.

'Didn't I warn you each time we met? You ignored my warnings and made fun of me and always narrated some foolish joke. But we will do everything possible to help you out. Keep your courage.'

Hanumant was a happy-go-lucky man. He was a well-paid executive in an international company. He played golf with his clients, took them to dinners in expensive restaurants and bagged contracts for his company. Living lavishly was a part of his job. He smoked expensive cigarettes and drank expensive drinks. He travelled in the best modes of conveyance around the corners of the world.

He had grown fat, for he hosted several lunches and dinners in a day for his clients. He hated exercise. He had neither any time nor inclination for walks. His joints creaked and cried as they failed to prop his bulk. He always reminded his critics that Winston Churchill neared hundred on his diet of cigars and brandy and Bal Bramhachariji, who lived on *shuddh* (pure) air and cow's curd left this world at the tender age of forty.

His jokes and wisecracks always irritated his friend, Dr Zhivago Naidoo. Strange name! Dr Zhivago was the only surviving child of his parents. To ensure survival, often a miserable name is appended to a baby. This keeps the devil in the dark. All his previous siblings had died either at birth or during infancy. When his mother conceived for the fifth time, his grandfather, a fan of Boris Pasternak, promised this name to his god.

Zhivago became a famous cancer surgeon. He led a healthy life. He took long walks, played tennis, and faithfully performed the asanas and pranayams, recommended by Soami Namdev. He recommended prayer to all his patients, ever since he read about its healing power in some medical journal. Like all important men, he too had a guru.

'I can go to London or anywhere in the US. Please advise me. Don't tell Regina about this. I will tell her in due course.' Regina was Hanumant's pretty wife; she was a Russian. Zhivago liked her immensely, and envied Hanumant's luck.

Zhivago imagined her as a sad widow. This profile seemed prettier to him. 'How fresh and beautiful she looks! Good she does not have children,' he mused on her plight.

'You needn't go anywhere. We will manage it here only. They have no magic cure over there.' Dr Zhivago gave a stern look and said, 'Regina told me that till yesterday you smoked cigarettes.'

'It was just one cigarette after lunch. I never thought for a moment that I would really have this. Pardon me, friend, doctors are next to God in healing and compassion. I am sure you will save me. From now on, I will comply with your advice, every single word of it. I promise. No breaches now.' Hanumant took a deep and sorrowful breath. 'Do not worry about the expenditure, my company will bear it all.'

Dr Zhivago's mind strayed again to Regina. By the way, he

was still a bachelor and was on a serious search for a good wife. He compared her to Mary Kutty and Katherine Abraham his latest interests. Mary was good from far but far from good. Katherine was good for only the bad purpose. Regina was far superior to both. She was a beautiful and sweet-natured woman; and despite her white skin, she had no pretensions. The only problem with her was her atrocious English; and that she smiled without any reason. It appeared odd sometimes.

'How long will I survive?' Hanumant rose from the sofa.

'Don't be so scared. What do you fear and why? Man never dies, he only changes his form and shape. You must read the Gita,' Zhivago solemnly advised.

'That means I am going to die for sure.' Hanumant closed his tearful eyes and lay down again.

'All of us are going to die for sure, it is not only you. Now you keep lying down. I will call my next patient. No interruption please!'

Death of cancer patients was a normal event for Zhivago. He accepted the fact and never found it strange. These events never upset him much. Zhivago pressed the bell to call in the next patient.

Hanumant decided not to listen to Zhivago's conversation with the other patient. Dr Zhivago examined and sent the patient away. Hanumant asked again boldly, 'How long do you think I will survive?'

'May be five years.'

Hanumant was filled with self-pity and a tear betrayed his eye.

'Why don't you join a course on the Art of Living? They help one to lose fear. They have a special course for cancer patients. You must turn your eyes inwards. God has actually given you a great opportunity to change your life. Take it this way,' the doctor advised.

Hanumant began weeping.

'I will give you two tapes, just listen to them. I have given these to many people. They feel at peace with themselves and life.'

'Which one is that? I too have a large collections of *bhajans* and spiritual tapes.' Hanumant wiped his tears.

'It is *mahamrityunjaya japa* and the chants of *om mani padme hum*. *Mahamritunjaya*, they say, either ends the end or facilitates it.'

'You are frightening me. Now I must go.' Hanumant got up to leave. Zhivago felt sad, embraced his friend and saw him off to the lift.

Death gradually tightens its dragnet and eventually brings each life to its proboscis. Each being is aware of this fact, and yet struggles to escape it. Zhivago felt a sense of amazement over the love of life people have. He recalled Yudhishthira's oft-quoted speech in the Mahabharata. 'Each being that takes birth dies without exception. Yet, his attitude towards the world is, as if he is going to live for ever; is the greatest of all wonders.'

Sunday being a holiday, Zhivago took a quick round of the ward, cheered up his patients and then left the hospital to meet Hanumant. Hanumant was slated for surgery on the coming Wednesday.

He found Hanumant at home, dictating his will to his attorney.

The two, then visited Zhivago's Guruji in Pune. The Guruji did not know Hanumant. He blessed Hanumant for a long life and prosperity. Hanumant felt very emotional and prostrated himself at the feet of the master. 'Guruji, bless me for a long and healthy life.'

'Of course, son! May God bless you!' The master placed his hand on Hanumant's head.

Hanumant felt happy and returned with a new hope for a long life. The blessing of a spiritual man cannot go wrong, he consoled himself.

Luckily the tumour was localised and had not spread. Zhivago successfully excised the spot and put Hanumant on chemotherapy. Hanumant's ordeal had ended well. At least five years were assured to Hanumant. Hanumant recovered his health and spirit fast. His attitude towards life and work went through a sea change. He excused himself from travelling that he was so fond of. He learned to relax and gave more time to himself. He developed newer hobbies, turned to books and golf with greater enthusiasm. He joined a voluntary society that helped in the rehabilitation of cancer patients. He developed a new poise and greater confidence. He appeared happier than before.

He turned to spirituality and God. Both, Guruji and Dr Zhivago, helped Hanumant to steer out of his depression and fear. The idea of death to him was no longer so fearsome. He became peaceful. His new life became a joy that he never experienced when he was healthier.

It was a Sunday in winter. Winter in Bombay is only on the calendar. The weather actually does not differ from summer months. After a golf session and coffee, Zhivago felt uneasy. Hanumant drove him home. Coffee did not flow down. It floated up to his mouth. Zhivago felt giddy. He threw up and felt better. The next day, he felt pain and stiffness in his neck and chest. He took leave and slept at home. His pain gradually increased. The following morning, he felt raw in his food pipe. Even cold water burnt his food pipe. He felt pain on swallowing. While shaving, he felt that his neck had swollen and veins were visible on his neck. He touched his neck and felt a swelling around his Adam's apple. It was warm. He caught the lump between his fingers. He tried to move it up and down and sideways. It remained stuck to where it was. Zhivago became panicky. His skill fled, he could not decipher it. He felt blank like a layman, only a bit more apprehensive.

He went to the hospital to see Mehta, his colleague. He never held Mehta, the other cancer surgeon, in high esteem. They were professional rivals. They missed no opportunity to pin each other down. Both had thought of leaving the Cancer Hospital several times after their tiffs and lack of support to them from the administration.

He smiled at Mehta. Mehta cautiously smiled back. 'Mehta, do you have some time today?' Zhivago again tried to smile.

'What do you want? You can come to my cabin at lunch time after I finish with my outpatients. Aren't you on leave?'

Zhivago was pacing outside Mehta's cabin; it seemed that Mehta was held up in his outpatient clinic. Mehta arrived long after the lunch hour was over, he beckoned Zhivago in.

'It seems to be a strange kind of inflammation to me,' Zhivago pointed to his neck. He appeared very impatient and agitated to Dr Mehta. Dr Mehta drew closer and looked at the swelling, palpated it, moved it and then asked him to swallow. Dr Zhivago, like an obedient and frightened patient followed all the instructions without question. Mehta laughed, 'It is nothing friend, but we will do a CT, a biopsy, thyroid function tests, that's all.'

'Why a CT, why a biopsy?' Zhivago stammered.

'We begin today itself. Why should a surgeon of this hospital wait for the next day? We do it now.' Mehta held Zhivago's hand and they walked to the department of Radiodiagnosis. Zhivago felt sick beyond words. He became panicky. His mouth dried. He was sweating.

Zhivago rang up Hanumant, 'Hanumant, I am not well, can you please come in the evening after your golf? I need you.'

Hanumant was there within an hour. 'What is the trouble my friend? You sound too panicky. You are a doctor. You cannot be ill.'

'I do not know Hanumant. I am really apprehensive. I fear for my life.' Zhivago closed his eyes and sighed.

The surgeon lay on the same bed in the intensive care unit as his patients used to. The one who played God, now begged for a few breaths. The man of knowledge seemed an unreasonable fool. Before the surgeon passed into coma, he laughed on this role reversal. He said that now his education was complete. He told Hanumant, 'The study of cancer was my passion, the goal of my life. Good, now I truly understand what cancer is. Bookish knowledge is too limited, Hanumant. To culminate the game of life the hunter should become the prey.'

Hanumant later told me that Dr Zhivago was diagnosed as a case of anaplastic carcinoma of the thyroid, the deadliest of the tumours. It spreads like wild fire and chews every bit of flesh in its way. There is no palliation for it.

Within four months of detection, the cancer snuffed the life out of Dr Zhivago.

□

The Schizophrenic

Harris Tuckerman was excited. He was going to India as a resource person and speaker in a writers' workshop at Mukteshwar, a small town in the Himalayas. He had heard a lot about the Himalayas, its mystics, yogis, tantrics and ghouls. The workshop was being organised by a publishing house, The Subtle Vision. Writers, mediums, and ghost-busters from across the borders, collected to share their experiences. Harris Tuckerman was a literary agent of horror fiction, but he actually never believed in the existence of spirits and ghosts. Their perception was only a sickness of the mind in his opinion.

Frankfurt airport was a walk through a pleasure garden. Invisible fairy lights, noiseless conveyer belts, smiling faces at the counters, pretty shops, soft music, the aroma of coffee and freshly baked cakes, and the revellers at restaurants, pleased his senses. Delhi airport stood in sharp contrast to its German counterpart. Passengers seemed to be in a hurry; they jostled out of the plane, and rushed into the corridor. A flood of strong fluorescent lights, along the passage to Immigration, jarred his sick eyes. He noticed the chipped wall-paint, shabby seats, and wilted plants in unpolished brass pots. A crudely forged brass figure of a woman greeted him with folded hands; it appeared like a shrivelled mummy.

There was chaos inside; everyone pushed others to report

at the Immigration, lest the immigration officers retired for the rest of the night. He too was gripped by a sense of panic. He too ran, following the riotous crowd.

The place was too hot. He removed his jacket and still sweated. A policeman ordered him to stand in a queue, and then asked him to join another. The policeman changed his mind again, and recalled him to the first one. Chaos overpowered him. He failed to understand why everybody at the Immigration and Customs seemed unhappy with him. They did not say anything rude to him, perhaps out of politeness, but not a soul smiled at him. He felt awful.

At the exit, a man held up a placard bearing his name. Harris dashed towards him. This man smiled and asked Harris to follow him. It was a December night. Outside was very cold; it was a sea of fog. Visibility was poor. He could barely see beyond three yards. Like light houses, yellow fog lights over tall, arched poles, gave a sense of location to the passengers.

Strangely, at that ungodly hour, he saw, or rather felt, a man astride the bend of a light pole. The man seemed to be wearing snow white clothes. However, the sight was not clear, for it was too foggy. The man was probably repairing something over there. It was too dangerous, he thought. He even doubted what he saw. He looked up again and felt a pair of tiny red eyes staring at him; that man even smiled.

Harris pointed the strange scene to the usher, and asked him who the man was and why he was on the pole at this hour. The usher kept silent, for he could not see anything except the fog light mounted on the pole. Harris became surprised when he again looked up, the man was not there. Harris opened his waist pouch, took out a plastic phial, and instilled medication into his eyes. His eye pressure dropped, and vision improved; he felt better.

They drove to Hotel Sultana, some twenty miles from the airport. It was still night. Harris checked in and lay in the bed. In the morning, Mr Randhava, the CEO of Subtle Vision, was to fetch him for a trip to Agra to visit the Taj. The next night they had to start their journey for the Himalayas. The month of December is quite cold in Delhi, the temperature drops as low as two degrees Celsius.

Harris woke up at eight in the morning, and drew open the curtains. The fog peered in through all the windowpanes. He could not see anything through the white fog. He skipped his bath, shaved and rushed out for breakfast. Not many visitors were present inside the lounge. Even in the breakfast room there were not many souls. He ordered an English breakfast, with orange juice, baked beans, omelette and ham.

He sat cosily on a cushioned chair, stretched a newspaper on the table, and sipped his coffee. Harris felt as if something had nudged his arms. His hands shook uncontrollably and the hot coffee spilled over his suit. A waiter rushed to him, wiped his suit and brought fresh coffee for Harris. The fog grew denser, it became darker. Florescent lights were switched on all over the place. Ignoring his involuntary tremors a few minutes ago, Harris quietly finished his coffee and returned to his room.

The telephone rang. Harris tried to reach the receiver. He felt that someone had clamped his forearm, and with great difficulty and force he could lift the instrument. Even while he brought it closer to his ears, he struggled with a powerful pull on his hand. Mr Randhava was on the other side. 'Mr Tuckerman welcome to India. How was your journey? Pleasant?'

'Good morning, Mr Randhava. Thank you. It is so wonderful here! I am waiting for you. Aren't you coming now?' The phone was pulled out of his hand and fell on the floor. Harris lifted the phone again. He began sweating because of the hard exercise of keeping the instrument in his hand. He became breathless owing to the extraordinary effort he was making against the power that was trying to snatch the instrument.

'Are you all right, Mr Tuckerman?'

'Yes, I am fine,' he gasped.

'Mr Tuckerman, the fog is very dense today and had spread all over the countryside. Till Agra and even beyond, the visibility is not more than a yard. We will not be able to drive that far, it is about two hundred kilometres from here. Moreover, unless the fog recedes one cannot see the Taj.'

'It is all right. I would like to rest today,' he managed to say before the instrument was snatched out of his hand. The telephone got disconnected. Harris lay on the bed, breathing heavily. He felt a strong presence of someone inside his room, but could not see anyone there. He looked out through the window pane; a white cloud ran across his window. He remembered his medication. He took out the phial and instilled a drop in each eye.

All that he did not believe in life, was happening to him. He found his things disappearing from their place. His spectacles lay in the wash basin.

Fortunately the next day, the fog had receded. They went to Agra, saw the Taj at noon, and returned to Delhi the same evening. They had to catch the train to Kathgodam.

The Ranikhet Express is a comfortable train with warmed coaches. It leaves Delhi around eleven at night, and reaches Kathgodam by six o'clock in the morning. Mukteshwar is a two-hour drive from Kathgodam. The train has many stops. People board and disembark throughout the journey. Unless one is endowed with an exceptional capacity to sleep, one keeps awake. The passengers buy sweet milky tea in disposable terracotta mugs at each halt, and noisily slurp it. Few could actually sleep.

Early in the morning, the heating failed, Randhava felt cold and woke up. He got down at a station, bought a mug of hot milky tea and returned to his coach. He found Harris sitting beside the window. He asked, 'Should I get you a cup of tea, Harris?'

Harris was peering out of the tainted window and perspiring. 'No thanks. Look, who is that man staring at me?' Harris pointed to a figure on the platform. Randhava could not see anyone on the deserted patch.

At Kathgodam, Harris told Randhava that he was not feeling well and needed a consultation. They took a detour, and drove to Haldwani to find a specialist in the district hospital. There, the ophthalmologist found Harris' eye pressure raised, he changed his medication. For his other complaints, the doctor advised Harris to see another doctor in the same hospital.

The other doctor, they discovered, was a psychiatrist. Though Harris was annoyed at this referral, he walked into the doctor's room and explained his symptoms.

'Did you experience these symptoms earlier?' the psychiatrist inquired.

'No, never,' Harris replied.

'Did any of your parents or grandparents suffer from any kind of anxiety or disturbance?'

'No, not to my knowledge, doctor.'

'Any of your uncles, aunts or siblings?'

'Not that I know of.'

'It is clearly a beginning of schizophrenia, Mr Tuckerman. I would like to observe you for a few days.'

'Sorry, I have come here for a meeting and have to return in a few days. I cannot prolong my stay here, doctor.' Harris felt offended by the diagnosis.

'We choose appropriate medicine and adjust the dose only by trial. For that we have to monitor patients. Drug induced complications are frequent. But if you want to travel, please do so at your own risk. Anyway, here are some pills for you to try.' The psychiatrist wrote the schedule of the drugs and their doses on a sheet of paper and handed over the prescription to Harris.

Randhava, who was sitting there, heaved a sigh of relief at Tuckerman's decision. The Subtle Vision had paid for Tuckerman's journey to India for the workshop. His absence from the meeting meant a loss to the company. The meeting was to begin the following day. They left for Mukteshwar the same evening. Randhava had booked a good hotel in the valley for the meeting.

For himself and his esteemed guest, he had hired another luxury hotel at the mountaintop.

The path to the hotel Hill Top was a narrow and uneven climb of one hour. Since the road was only six feet wide, one could only walk or ride on horseback. The road was cut through steep rocks. On one side of the road, were the rocks, and the other side dipped almost perpendicularly into a thousand feet deep gorge. Trees hid the gorge from sight, at places it was visible. Any mistake was fatal. Many drunken men had disappeared into the gorge. Harris and Randhava drove up in a tiny horse carriage up to the hotel. The night in the hotel was comfortable. Harris was on heavy sedation, he slept well.

The day began well. Tuckerman made a flawless presentation on the principles of writing horror tales and the power of imagination and words. 'Actual disbelief of the author in the supernatural is a plus point, as it gives him a sense of objectivity, and renders his tale believable,' he told the gathering.

A number of presentations by the tantra adepts, practitioners of dark arts and the worshippers of corpses were made. Their appearances and accounts chilled the marrow of the listeners. It was indeed a unique workshop.

'Imagination creates,' a suave practitioner of black magic declared. He was a remarkable man, short, strong and muscular. He exuded a cold sense of power. His phrases and sentences were interspersed with long spells of silence. His sentences were not well connected and coherent. He thought for long before speaking as if he waited for the sentences to emerge from somewhere. Harris felt that he was translating and interpreting someone invisible.

The man waved his torso and gesticulated with his hands. The windows of the room flapped. He raised his effort, and the windows flung open sucking in white clouds. 'Hark', he shouted, the wolves howled somewhere. He raised his hands up and pulled some invisible strings in the air, kites gathered in the sky. He pulled a few down. They nosedived and perched on the window sills. At the end he scrubbed the air to erase an invisible graffiti. The illusion disappeared. The windows seemed closed as before. There was no trace of the unusual events that Harris experienced, a few moments ago. Harris could not believe his eyes and ears. Was it the arousal of clairvoyance and clairaudience lying dormant in him or was he becoming insane? He looked at the others. They were listening to the speaker with rapt attention. He wondered whether they too experienced the same. The magician smiled at Harris.

He spoke, 'An acute observation, a happening around life that interests you, can make an interesting story. You may blow up a simple incident with your language skill and contrive a story.'

He became silent for long and then spoke again. 'Books are there, they are conscious in their own domain. They look for an author the same way an author searches a theme and plot.'

After a prolonged silence he resumed. 'The unwritten novels and stories float in a world of mind. An author happens to pass through them. One of these may fit into the groove of his mind, like a key in the lock. Upon engagement with a corresponding hiatus, the book empties its contents into it.'

'Sometimes, a power possesses you. It speaks through you. Some beings take possession of a capable mind, and make him write their own story. Angels, fairies, gnomes, goblins, giants and other creatures come with their tales and pass it to an author without his knowledge. The world and character of the dispenser, is reflected in the story. The author is then, merely a medium.

'There is a mart of wizards. It has a story lane in it. The shopkeepers sit with small beautiful velvety bundles—black, silver, cherry red, orange, blue, green, and golden—each contains either a novel or a story, or even a poem. Generally, the passers-by in this charmed alley are the story-tellers and poets. They are presented those parcels. They may accept, or bargain for another. Therein lay an unformed poem or the essence of a story, for developing, pruning and sprucing it up.

'Often a Santa Claus-like being passes on his sleigh drawn by his seven reindeers. He bestows gifts to the spectators who stand along his trail. Authors may find tender saplings of novels and stories. They are to be watered and raised, and then shaped with industry to a handsome form.'

Harris, now noticed a strange man standing by the speaker's side. He reminded Harris of the man over the fog light pole. But this time he was in a black robe. Harris felt frightened. He suddenly realised that he had not taken his morning dose of sedation. He took out his pills and swallowed, and instilled his eye drops. He felt better within a quarter of an hour. The man too had disappeared by then.

The speaker finished and sat next to him. He was actually a tantrik and had authored a few books on tantra. The speaker indicated to Harris that he wanted to talk to him. But Harris put his fingers on his own lips, signalling the man to keep silent. The man smiled and stood up. He said, 'All right, I will see you later. You seem to be tired. Sleep.' The man walked out of the hall. Harris closed his eyes and slept till the end of all the speeches.

Randhava woke him up, they had to walk back to the hotel. The speaker had returned and sat close to them. He wanted to speak to Harris. He urged, 'I must speak to you Mr Tuckerman.'

Harris still felt tired and sleepy. 'Can't you see me tomorrow? I am not well. I must go.'

The man felt disappointed, 'Tomorrow I will not be here. I must leave tonight. It is about a manuscript. It is important that I speak to you now.'

Harry lost his temper, he curtly answered, 'You may write to me, all you want to say.' He got up and patted Randhava, 'Let's go.'

Harris was trying to avoid the Indian writers. Some of them had flocked around him at the lunch hour to solicit his help in publishing their manuscripts. He could barely manage to munch his sandwich. Indians expected to make it big by publishing abroad. Harry had become wary of them.

Randhava and Harris walked back to their hotel. Harris felt very unnatural. He felt very light; he felt that that the earth had lost its gravitational pull, and he walked inches above. His movements overreached his intention and effort.

It had become dark. Suddenly, Harris saw a horse galloping past through him, as if he was made of thin air. The man whom he saw at the fog light pole, and then at the conference with the speaker, was mounting the horse. He was amazed that Randhava could not sense anything unusual. Randhava suggested that they should walk faster; Harris needed rest; the sedation was playing tricks in Harris' mind, Randhava suggested.

They took a long time to reach the hotel. Randhava helped Harris to find his room. Harris took his medication and fell like a log over his bed. Randhava came to call him for dinner, he knocked, Harris was fast asleep.

In the middle of the night Harris woke up. The weather had become pleasant. It was warmer. He felt fresh and cheerful. There was no fog outside. Moonlight bathed the scenery. Snow-clad mountains looked beautiful. He sat at the window to admire the panorama.

He heard a knock at the door. He went and opened the door. The speaker was there with the man Harris feared. But this time Harris felt no fear. He welcomed both of them in. They entered and sat on the chairs. No one spoke. After some time Harris asked the speaker, 'Have you brought the manuscript? I can finalise it right away. We need stories and I'm sure I will find a publisher for you.'

'Thank you, I have not come for that. Haven't you met Mr Ram?' The other man smiled. He looked somewhat strange, for he did not look quite solid. He appeared like a man made of fluid.

'Is Mr Ram also an author?' Harris enquired.

'Yes, he was. Mr Ram had sent you a story book when he

was alive.' The speaker informed Harris.

'Did he? I do not remember that,' Harris said.

'The name of the book was *The World of the Dead.* Didn't you publish the book in your own name after the death of Mr Atma Ram?' The speaker smiled.

Harris jumped out of his skin. 'Atma Ram!' He screamed.

'Now, you talk to Mr Ram. He has come to see you in this regard.' Both the guests stood up. Atma Ram raised his hand and snapped his fingers. The speaker moved to the window, opened it and walked out on air, and disappeared.

Atma Ram stared at Harris, his eyes had a red glint. He said nothing. Harris' heart pounded. He felt that he would soon lose consciousness. He was scared to death. Ram kept staring at Harris, till his figure gradually decomposed into a dark miasma.

Harris ran towards the door, it was locked from outside. The window was over a cliff, he dared not jump out. He retraced his steps. An arm arising out of the amorphous matter pulled him towards itself. Now Harris was in it, as if engulfed by it. He was sucked deeper into a black hole.

Harris shrieked in horror. His shriek was quenched in the black mass. No one heard his screams at night. He ran and swam inside the tarry mass for long but could not find his way out, nothing was visible. It was all pitch dark and too thick. He fell exhausted on his bed. His body became stiff, and pained. He writhed in agony. Like a poisoned fly in a spider's web, his motion gradually stilled. The horror sapped his life drop by drop till he was lifeless like an empty shell.

Harris was discovered dead in the morning. The police were informed. The body was sent for post-mortem. The blood and the contents of the bowels suggested an overdose of sedatives. The case was solved without any difficulty. It was a simple case and closed as such. His body was posted to his wife.

□

Black Ivy

'Hadn't you been my best friend, I wouldn't have shared these beautiful secrets with you. Now, hold your ears, and promise that you will never tell this to anyone, including Aniruddh.'

'All right, all right!' I held my ears to his contentment, and urged him, 'Now tell.'

'Ivy was the most beautiful girl that I ever saw. She was as dark as ebony. No! Ebony is not the right word; I would say, as dark as black gold. Her skin glowed like blue Krishna. She wore no makeup to lighten her colour. She was just beautiful. When she smiled she looked gorgeous, and when cried, she looked even better. She never believed me when I told her she was so pretty. Her mother also lamented her skin colour. She said that it would be difficult to marry off her daughter easily,' Dhananjaya told me.

'Dhananjaya, it could be your own inner feeling rather than her beauty.'

'No Rahul, all the boys agreed to this fact. She was the darling of the boys, the girls were jealous of her. We studied together till the eighth class in the Rajghat School. Then her mother moved her to an all girls' school, a Bengali school. She was against the coeducational system in the higher classes. We have not met since.'

'All right, find her this time when you go home for the summer vacations. If you wish, I too may come with you.' I was charmed by the idea of her beauty.

May and June are the hottest months of the year. The medical school closed, all the students went home. Varanasi was not far from Lucknow. A night train was available for Mughal Sarai which was 15 kms from Varanasi. The two of us reached the city like excited archaeologists on a mission to excavate a historical monument in Damascus.

The sun shone high in the sky by nine o'clock, and baked the earth. The tar melted over the roads. Hot winds, called *loo*, violently blew over the town. Birds hid themselves in trees. Buffaloes and urchins swam in ponds and puddles. The vagabonds took shelter on the ghats under bamboo parasols, or along the shadows of citadels on the river bank. Charitable souls all over the town, offered drinking water to the thirsty. After six in the evening, there was some respite from the heat.

We had limited time, we thought of not losing it. We perspired under the scorching sun to search her house. Each day, we returned exhausted because my friend had forgotten the lane in which she lived. The city is a cobweb of lanes within lanes, like the capillaries of a pipul leaf. We walked through these four feet wide alleys; they never seemed to end. At the end of the day, we found ourselves either, miles away from where we began, or surprisingly, almost next to the beginning.

Parents used to be very protective those days. Unlike today, they were allowed to beat even a forty-year-old. They remained the ultimate authority over the lives of their children till their end. One evening, my twenty-two-year-old friend was slapped by his father on the charge of loafing around at noon. I too felt scared as I was staying with him. Those days, even beating a son's friend was no offence. My parents would have appreciated such treatment as a sign of good care and concern. The guest was never discriminated against nor made to feel left out, he used to be treated as a member of the immediate family. Thereafter, we decided to study during the daytime and look for Ivy after sunset.

One evening, near the Rama temple in the old city, Dhananjaya spotted an old friend, Cheeku. He was a school dropout and lived near Ivy's house. He did odd jobs in the shops of the lane, and also worked as an usher for the night shows in a cinema hall. We watched a Bollywood movie with him, of course for free. He gave Dhananjaya Ivy's new address. We were very happy to find her address.

It was past midnight. We rushed back home. Dhananjaya's father did not like 'children' to stay out after ten at night. He firmly believed that only the rogues stayed out that late. We got back by two o'clock and sneaked into the house. Mercifully, the father was sound asleep after his night dose of *bhang*[1].

From the rich Chaukhambha lane, Ivy had shifted to Sonarpura. Sonarpura is an ancient locality on the bank of the Ganga. Most of its inhabitants are poor Bengalis. Their rich ancestors had made beautiful houses on the bank of the river to spend their last days in peace. With time, everything decays including man, stone and lime.

The next evening, we loitered from lane to lane in Sonarpura. The buildings were ancient, plaster had peeled off, bricks were exposed and decaying, dung cakes were drying over the walls. There were a few new houses, cheaply built. Kalimandir Lane in Sonarpura was a mottled dusty track with tar plaster at places. There was no light because of the power cuts. There were several roadside four by four feet dimly-lit temples, which illuminated small stretches of the lane. Cattle and rodents wandered all over. They had no fear of man, men feared them.

Finally we located the house in an unnamed side lane. We found a small grocery stall at the entrance of a small, double storeyed house. An open sewer separated the shop and the pavement. The customers stood cautiously on the pavement. There was no space to stand inside.

The shop was generally dark; a tiny oil lamp was lit in it. A serene girl with a lovely face sat beside the lamp. A little boy helped her pack goods. Now, I was left with little doubt that she was the Ivy we were looking for, indeed the most beautiful face I ever saw. I instantly agreed with Dhananjaya. 'Dhananjaya, she is angelic. God has sculpted her with his own hands.' I was charmed. On a longer look, I discerned a streak of deep sorrow in her large eyes that radiated to her face. The sorrow made her face haunting.

When the shoppers dispersed, we walked to the stall. Ivy, without looking at Dhananjaya asked, 'May I help you, sir?'

'Ivy!' Dhananjaya shouted in excitement. 'Don't you remember me? I am Dhananjaya.'

Her face brightened, 'Dhananjaya!' she cried. 'It's you?' Her eyes widened and she smiled at the sudden surprise. 'You are a big doctor now, Cheeku told me.' Ivy giggled happily looking at Dhananjaya. For a brief moment the sorrow left her face.

'Big doctor? I am still a student, Ivy.'

Ivy asked her brother to take us up, and prepare tea while she closed the shop. The brother, a sweet kid knocked at the side door and shouted, 'Ma, ma.' Someone pulled the string attached to the latch, the latch opened with a click. The boy pushed the door open and we climbed a dark staircase holding the wall. The house was only a room on the second floor.

His mother asked from inside, 'Khokun, have you finished with the shop?'

'Dhananjaya *da*[3] has come.' The boy said enthusiastically in Bengali. It seemed that he probably had heard his sister speak of Dhananjay sometime. The door opened, and his mother welcomed us in.

Ivy's mother was cooking. The room was full of spicy aromas. Though dimly lit by a kerosene lamp, the room looked shabby. It is more difficult to tidy a small place than a big house. Dhananjaya touched her feet. The mother smiled happily and exclaimed, 'Dhananjaya! You have become so big! You were so small when I saw you last. Have you started shaving?' She caressed his cheeks, 'I hear you are a big doctor now.'

'*Masima*[3] I am only a student, not a big doctor.'

'You will become a big doctor,' the mother laughed.

'Who is this?' She asked about me.

'Rahul, my class fellow.'

She pulled up two chairs, and made place for us to sit. The house reeked of unmitigated poverty. The mother prepared tea. The brother brought a stool and placed it in front of us to keep our teacups. He raised the wick of the kerosene lamp to brighten the room.

'Why did you leave Chaukhambha house, *Masima*?' Dhananjaya asked.

'It was too expensive. Khokun was born after his father's death. We had no choice. Here the rents are low and food is cheap. This area is good and secure. Bengali widows live here. The river is only half a mile from here. What more do we need?'

In a few minutes, Ivy walked in; she sat down on a *charpoy* opposite us. She looked happy in her sadness. She spoke little, and shyly watched Dhananjaya talking to her mother. After we finished the tea, she insisted on more. We finished the second cup.

Masima told Dhananjaya that she stitched clothes at a shop to make ends meet. Her only worries were Khokun's education and Ivy's marriage. She lamented, 'It is difficult to find a groom for a dark girl.'

After an hour or so, we asked her permission to leave. 'Come again Dhananjaya. Pay my respects to your father and mother. Good souls! They must have done penance in their past life to get a son like you.' She embraced Dhananjaya affectionately.

Ivy and her brother came down to see us off. We walked till the rickshaw stand. 'Come again Dhananjaya,' Ivy pleaded.

'I will,' Dhananjaya promised.

We came back home. Dhananjaya was very sad to see the condition of Ivy's house. 'It used to be a rich household at Chaukhambha. Visitors were always there. *Masima* used to wear silk saris and a thick line of vermillion in her parting. She too was very good looking. The little brother was not born then.' I heard Dhananjaya with curiosity and asked several questions about them.

'I would have married Ivy, had I been independent, and of her caste. We are Kanyakubja Brahmins of Kannauj, and they are Bengali Brahmins. They eat fish. It is impossible for us,' Dhananjaya sighed.

We again visited Ivy before returning to Lucknow. Indeed, Ivy was the most beautiful girl. Her sadness haunted me. I thought of her in Lucknow. When Dhananjaya came back from Varanasi after the next vacation, I asked about Ivy.

'They have left that house too. This time even Cheeku does not know their new address. Actually, Cheeku had gone to them to borrow some money. *Masima* always gave him something. He was very disappointed.' We felt sad to have lost track of Ivy again.

After a heavy day, Dhananjaya and I decided to relax that evening, and have a cup of coffee at the Royal Café. It was a cool and pleasant evening. We strolled past the Church at Hazratganj (in Lucknow). An Ambassador car suddenly stopped a few yards away, and then it reversed back with great speed, and stopped within inches from us. It was a close shave, very annoying. Before we could protest at the rudeness of the driver, a woman yelled out of the car window, 'Dhananjaya.' Reality astonishes more than stories.

She was Ivy. She looked happily married. She had a little baby in her arms. Her husband, Sukanto, was the son of Gouri Ghosh, the famous distributor of Bollywood movies in the north. They insisted, and we happily accompanied them to Royal Café. We had a sumptuous dinner. Sukanto did all the talking.

Ivy appeared serene through her sorrow. She spoke little but looked happier. She pointed us to her fair and lovely child, 'Dhananjaya and Rahul *mama*[4]. Say *mama* child.' She turned to Dhananjaya, 'Dhananjaya, look, she is so fair. I am happy. Girls should be fair. When I was pregnant my only prayer to God was to give me a fair child. God heard me. It is easier to marry off a fair daughter.' She smiled. Sukanto said, 'No fairness can match my black Ivy.'

Dhananjaya and I completed our studies, and went our ways in the pursuit of our respective careers. We married, I a girl of my own choice. Dhananjaya married a Brahmin girl selected by his mother.

Years have passed and we are here in time today. Even today, all of us are good friends. Whenever we are in Lucknow we meet at Ivy's house. She is still very pretty. The tinge of sorrow and humility never abandoned her face and smile, it is still there. Khokun is well settled. He is a musician and teaches at Bhatkhande University of Music. *Masima*, though old, looks elegant in silk saris.

Even at the age of fifty-nine our wives, Sukanto, Dhananjaya and I believe, 'No fairness can match our black Ivy.'

This is a story, too common to be shared, had Ivy not been in it.

□

---

1. Bhang is an intoxicant prepared from hemp leaves.
2. Short of Dada, address for an elder brother.
3. Means aunt in Bengali.
4. Address for maternal uncle.

Honesty Pays

Honesty is the best policy, someone great, probably Gandhiji, said that in the past century. A sub divisional magistrate (SDM), oath bound to protect the Constitution of India and the laws of his state, also believed in this motto like all civil servants of India swear.

Hindu names are often beautiful and lofty. They give a man his ideal of life. On the other hand, this too is true that most men become the opposite of their names. Sitaram may be an atheist, Dharma a criminal, Nainsukh blind and Lakshmi a pauper. The magistrate was Mr Vairagi. This Sanskrit name refers to a man who has renounced worldly pleasures.

He was recently posted in the Pinjore town of Balmora district. This town in the Himalayas is famous for its temples and soapstone mines. Soapstone is used to produce talcum powder. These mines are the property of respective temples scattered all over the town.

These days, people have lost their religious fervour and interest. The pilgrims have become miserly, they make little offerings to the temples. It has become fashionable to offer donations to income tax-exempted non-governmental-organisations and charities. In such fallen times, the priests have little choice; mines have become more profitable than the temples. Not that, they do not offer services to the pilgrims and deities, they have diversified to mining. They do not depend on pilgrims any more.

They are better off now. The priests now have cars, heated houses and access to modern amenities. Their children go to the English medium schools and speak English at home. They drive to Balmora and Nainital for McDonald's fast food.

It is astonishing, how the study of history provides us with the perspective of a contemporary reality, and corrects our misconceptions. For example, bribe is not a dirty word once we learn of its august origin. In ancient times, the sovereign used to distribute his territory to the local tsars. They had to take care of the subjects, earn their own living and also pay tribute to the crown in cash. They had no resources other than their territory and subjects, whose labour and offerings met their obligations. The emperor never paid them anything for their services to him.

In the contemporary context, we all know that the government hires its officers for salaries which are considered nothing, but an honorarium of sorts by them. The pundits have researched and found, that these people are willing to work for their employer without any remuneration, and that they are even willing to buy a job if auctioned by the government. Why? To serve the people and government, silly.

In the year 2007, before the implementation of the new scales, Mr Vairagi used to get a salary of rupees 20,000 a month, virtually nothing to match the lifestyle of the miners. How could a regent of the government rule under such circumstances? The suzerain would be reduced to a dignified office guard, or clerk at the most. Our new found democracy may end up in chaos, and Burmese rule may follow this time. In the face of such a grave eventuality, it falls on the patriotic citizens to provide for the local civil servants and save the country. This ancient practice of the upkeep of officers by the people has time-honoured wisdom in it: it establishes the respect for the government in the minds of people, it upholds essential decorum, and facilitates the rule of law and suzerain.

A young and ambitious priest who wanted always to be in the good books of the government officials, called on the new magistrate. That day, Mr Vairagi was in a sullen mood. His mood became worse glancing at the small basket of seasonal fruit, the priest had brought with him. The priest was very garrulous.

However, Mr Vairagi's mood improved after the preliminaries. They turned into long-lost friends, for they had several common acquaintances including the previous SDM. The priest spoke ill of him. The previous SDM, Mr Nanhe Khan, was a thoroughly corrupt man and did not care for human values. He shamelessly asked for bribes. Mr Vairagi changed the subject and asked the young priest, 'Are you married?'

'No Sir, not yet. Sir, I do not ever intend to commit this nuisance, not even in future. I am trying to expand my business in France, Sir.'

'Then you would never understand.' Mr Vairagi sighed deeply.

'Sir, what is that I would never understand?'

'The plight of married men.' The SDM smiled sadly.

'Sir, can I be of any help to you and your plight, Sir?' The priest humoured the SDM.

'No my dear, you can't be of any help. For me honesty is next to God.' Mr Vairagi, under his own spell, returned the worthless basket.

The young man returned impressed by the new Sahib. He spoke well of the SDM to one and all. Mr Vairagi's reputation spread over the town. An ill-conceived admission of honesty became a millstone around his neck that pulverised all the pleasures due to him as the SDM of the area. People were scared to offer him bribes. Though their jobs were occasionally stalled by the SDM for no clear reason, it never occurred to them to bribe him. They stretched Mr Vairagi's admission a bit too far.

Despite the damage caused to him, Mr Vairagi enjoyed the company of this young and humorous man. They continued meeting and chatting and occasionally gossiping about others.

Another day, Mr Vairagi sighed again, 'You won't understand?'

'What Sir?'

'The plight of married men.'

'Sir, why do you presume so? Even if I have not married, Sir, I have participated in many weddings and observed several married couples. Tell me, Sir, if I can, I will do my best to make you happy, Sir. I can not bear to see you gloomy. Just confide in me, Sir.'

'Friend, I will; I have no other choice now.' Mr Vairagi seemed exasperated with his situation. 'The cause of my suffering is my honesty. You see I have vowed to remain honest.'

'Sir, I agree with you. Honesty is the best policy Sir.' The priest encouraged the SDM.

Mr Vairagi stammered, but then managed to boldly say, 'You see, my wife comes from a rich family. She is the daughter of a rich man. She is accustomed to all kinds of luxuries, and she says she can not live in Pinjore. The house is not yet furnished. The plastic dining table looks so cheap that she is ashamed to take her meals on it. There is no TV at home, no movie hall in the town. For movies, she has to go to Balmora and has to depend on her father to send his car. I sometimes feel like committing suicide, brother. Neither can I become rich like her father nor become a hypocrite like DM (district magistrate) Sahib. I am a man who lives entirely within his means. You know I have vowed to remain honest.'

The priest's eyes widened. He had never been to DM Sahib, who seldom came from Balmora. The priest thought that he had come across some secret treasure. He asked in a conspiratorial tone, 'What does DM Sahib do? I have heard that Mr Sly is a very upright officer and a religious man. He spends all his time with holy men and visits the Shiva temple of Balmora every day.'

'Then you don't know enough about Mr Rajinder Singh Sly. He is crooked as a cork screw.' Mr Vairagi snorted. 'He has made a temple inside his own house. The businessmen visit his temple more than they visit the Shiva temple in the town. They placate his family deity, make offerings to her with their names written on the parcels.

'Surely, Mr Sly deals with bribe givers with an iron hand. One or two who wanted to negotiate money matters directly with him without the mediation of his deity, were arrested. He plainly says that he has no interest in worldly matters, but he does not mind if someone offers his heart at the feet of his deity. Rather, he minds if someone doesn't.' Mr Vairagi insinuated and laughed at his own clever speech. 'He says that he has nothing to do with what goes on between a devotee and the deity. That is a private matter between the two.'

The priest noted each word of Mr Vairagi in his mind, for they were the words of worldly wisdom. They offered a great possibility and insight into dealing with senior officers. A great mystery was revealed to him by the SDM Sahib. He had read in the Gita that each action of life could be offered to the divine and thus spiritualised. But it never occurred to him that dishonesty too could thus be spiritualised. A new possibility leered at him.

'It is anyone's guess, what happens to that money. But be sure, in case the offering falls short of his expectation, the devotee's desire is never fulfilled. Bloody rogue, hypocrite!' Mr Vairagi laughed derisively. 'Nobody could touch the registrar of Land and House Sale and Transfer Deeds. A hundred complaints were made to Mr Sly, he rebuked the complainants. The registrar is the greatest devotee of Mr *Sly's* goddess.'

'I see.' The priest gasped in the light of the revelation. 'My God, what has our country come to?' the priest asked himself. 'To mix religion with corruption is the most dangerous cocktail,' he said.

'Exactly!' Mr Vairagi solemnly agreed with him. That made the priest happy with his own original thinking.

'Well, that is not the end. He has several tricks up his sleeve. Last year, when I was in Dameshwar, He called a meeting of all the important businessmen and told them, "I want to make this annual religious fair of Bameshwar, a tourist attraction. Tourists mean, better employment opportunities for our boys, and cash in the coffers of the town. I would like to create a website too to attract tourists from all over the world, including the rich Western countries. Let us put Bameshwar on the north pole of the spiritual world.

"Sir, a website will not be enough, we must have other ways of publicity too," a crony crooned.

"Exactly, this is what I have thought. The government has sanctioned only fifty thousand rupees for the fair. We would need four lakhs and fifty thousand more in case we want to have cultural programmes. We can invite top dancers from outside, and pay them." DM Sahib responded to the suggestion.

"We are prepared to pay the balance, Sir. We are grateful to you for such a fantastic idea. Our Bameshwar would be the North Pole of the spiritual world under your dynamic leadership." The man applauded Mr Sly.

"That's a great idea. We will meet the shortfall. The money will reach you tomorrow, Sir," the businessmen assured Mr Sly.

'The meeting concluded. The next day the traders went to the DM's office with cash, and placed it on his table. Mr Sly looked shocked and displeased; it smacked of corruption to him. He had no personal advantage in Bameshwar being on top of the world. He chided them, and asked them to take away their cash and make the payments in cheques and drafts to the treasury officer of the district. Every transaction should be on record and be transparent. He had no personal gain in the matter, he thundered.'

The priest listened quietly and made a mental note.

'Won't you ask, what he did with the money?' Mr Vairagi roused the priest's curiosity.

'What did he do?' the priest asked with curiosity.

'He called his sister and her gang of musicians from Patna, his mother and brother included. They came by a chartered helicopter. The troupe stayed in Hotel Shikhar of Balmora. They came to Bameshwar just for two hours, hurriedly gave a performance and rushed back the same evening to Balmora. They had a charity concert at Balmora the next evening. In Balmora, the seats were sold for two hundred rupees each; each seat was sold out. The hall was jam-packed. Later, they gave a programme at Dehradun. The chief minister was invited. Would you believe that the next year the chief minister awarded the Gandharva Award, the state's highest for music, to Mr Sly's sister.'

'My God.' The priest was awed by Mr Sly's cleverness.

'Men like me always suffer because they are honest. Our wives taunt us, and run away. There is no domestic happiness, my dear.' Mr Vairagi sighed, and closed his eyes in remorse. The priest looked at him with sympathy.

The priest passed a detailed account of the domestic unhappiness of the new SDM to his colleagues. They were sad about the upright man. The community felt that an honest officer should not suffer on account of honesty, a virtue next to God. They instantly collected money.

A truck unloaded, a dining table set with chairs, furnishings for all the rooms including bed sheets, a refrigerator, microwave oven and kitchen wares, a plasma TV with home theatre, a washing machine and a laptop computer, at the SDM's house.

Only after the traders vouched and convinced Mr Vairagi that they were presenting those items as his blood brothers, and not at all as traders, did he accept their gifts. They reiterated that they had no dishonest expectations from him in return for the booty they offered.

'Honesty pays,' Mr Vairagi mused lolling on his rocking chair.

□

The Tribals

Mr Dhritiman Mahapatra, Dhriti or sometimes Dirtyman, to his buddies, was a retired Secretary to the Government of India. He was originally from Orissa, but had decided to spend his remaining years in Delhi, the city of opportunity for retired bureaucrats. He used to get consultancies. Currently, he was chief executive officer of four companies and received his salaries from each of them. Each company had provided him a car and a chauffeur. Though he had a sprawling house in Gurgaon, he preferred to stay in a company-owned house in Panchsheel, an upmarket colony of Delhi. He still had access to ministries of Finance and Commerce. He always got wind of new proposals in advance. That was why the companies made him their CEO, though he really never spent time with them. He was mostly seen in the corridors of ministries during the day and the India International Centre in the evenings; he never dined at home. His wife always accompanied him, except on some sensitive occasions. He was never tired of women, wealth and wine. He was proud of the fact that he was voted as the most corrupt officer by his fellow creatures. He was regularly named in scams and scandals but skilfully walked over all the storms. He rose like a sphinx and grabbed all the plum postings on his way to the top. A Prime Minister found him fit to become Cabinet Secretary but the jealousy of the competitors called a halt to his further rise.

None of his children from two wives showed their father's

brilliance. The son from his late wife was a drunkard and drug addict. He was over forty years and never could settle down. His wife had left him. He lived somewhere in the US. The daughter was a student, naturally, in the US.

Life passed well year after year; the time was catching up with him. The seventieth birthday is an important landmark in a man's life. This was also the day he married his present wife of twenty-five years. Kiron claimed to be a poetess; few could disagree with her assertion (for the sake of courtesy). She was the daughter of an Education Secretary, who died thirty years ago and ex-wife of a retired Foreign Secretary. Mr Mahapatra was her second husband. She took extra care for this marriage to flourish. She had written a book of poetry for this occasion, and her book was to be released by Sanguine Publishers in the Hotel Taj, the same evening. Eight hundred guests with their spouses were invited, including politicians, bureaucrats, diplomats, industrialists, culture honchos, famous artists, writers, poets and eminent citizens. A minister released the book. Cocktails made the rounds. A Bollywood starlet danced to a current tune, titillating the audience. Beautiful women and powerful men flirted with each other, fixed dates, appointments and business.

Police had taken over the internal traffic of the hotel. A large posse of policemen was awe inspiring. It spoke of the influence of Mr Mahapatra, though retired. An ancient proverb says that a dead elephant is worthier than a living one. The party proved it.

An inconspicuous figure, a policeman from Chattisgarh, had mingled among the crowd of his Delhi brothers. They asked him, why he was there. He did not answer. He accepted a cold drink and watched the revelry.

Mrs Mahapatra left with her daughter around midnight. The policeman kept a sharp eye on Mr Mahapatra. He waited in the cold till three in the morning, when after seeing off an inebriated minister, Mr Mahapatra moved towards his car. He looked in the side mirror, combed his hair. He looked good and fresh. He took out a cigar case from his pocket, and pulled one out. His driver lit a matchstick to help Mr Mahapatra. The cigar was lit. Mr Mahapatra drew a deep puff and released the jet of smoke into the cold air. He stooped to enter the car. The policeman who waited for the moment tapped his shoulders. 'A moment please, Sir.'

Mahapatra stopped and looked back at the imprudent man. It was a petty police officer. He could read his low designation from the chevron on his shoulder and his cap. Mr Mahapatra felt offended by the tap on his shoulder. 'A small man!' he thought.

'What do you want?' Mr Mahapatra snapped with familiar contempt that the bureaucrats of India, even the retired ones, exhibit towards the mortals of this country.

The policeman lifted up his cap in the cold. 'Sir,' the man hesitated realising his puny position. He passed a paper to Mr Mahapatra. 'What is this?'

'Summons,' the police man said.

'Which court?' Mr Mahapatra asked. He was accustomed to courts in connection with his work.

'Bilaspur,' the man answered.

'Bilaspur?' Mr Mahapatra raked his mind. 'What has Bilaspur to do with me now? I was the DM (district magistrate) there over thirty years ago. Come tomorrow to my office. I am too tired,' Mr Mahapatra told the police officer.

'Sir, I have been trying to meet you for the last few days without success.'

'Come tomorrow at 3 pm.' Mr Mahapatra got into his car and pulled the door. The car sped away.

Mr Mahapatra felt disturbed the whole night, though he was accustomed to such strange happenings as a district officer and later as commissioner. At this stage of life why should a judicial officer summon him to Bilaspur? He was out of Bilaspur for over thirty years now.

He should have seen the summons. He made a mistake, he felt.

The next day he went to the office, a room in his residence. He was still sleepy. He had three meetings in the afternoon, one at three pm. He asked his secretary to cancel the meeting. The policeman came promptly at three. He made the man wait for half an hour, while he read the newspaper. The officer gave the document to his secretary, took a receipt, and left. At half past three when Mr Mahapatra summoned the officer, he had gone out of reach.

The summons was from the Tribal Commission in connection with a complaint filed by a tribal organisation. There were no further details. Mr Mahapatra felt troubled. He made several telephone calls to important people in Delhi to find out about the current district magistrate of Bilaspur. By the evening, he could locate him. The young district magistrate was Sadananda Mahapatra. Dhriti was delighted to note that the DM belonged to his own caste. Mr Sadananda Mahapatra was a young man, around thirty-five years old, unmarried. He found his telephone number and rang him the next day. The young man appeared rude given the age of Mahapatra Senior, and the position he retired from. Mr Mahapatra knew enough tact to deal with such people.

Dhriti reached Bilaspur, stayed at the circuit-house, the official guest house for the top government officers and ruling politicians. The next day, Mr Mahapatra made a phone call to the collector's office. The DM was not available. His secretary informed Dhriti that under the circumstances the latter need not visit the DM. He showed scant regard for Mr Mahapatra's persona and position. It was most regrettable, that the young men in the elite service should behave with their predecessors in that manner. He felt snubbed and insulted.

In his days, the secretaries, serving or retired were treated over and above all the gods by everyone, including the junior officers of the elite services. He recalled how well Mr Tiwari, a retired ICS officer who had settled in Bilaspur, was treated by all the officers of the district. He and the superintendent of police were always available when Mr Tiwari called. Mr Tiwari was never made to feel retired. They made him live like a feudal lord in Bilaspur. Men of their service had precedence over the ministers in the past. In a tiff with the Secretary, the Home Minister had to go. Mr Nehru had accepted the resignation of Mr Gulzarilal Nanda. Times have changed. He lamented the decline of standards of the present-day officers. The present generation was setting a bad example for their juniors to follow. He visualised the destruction of their ivory tower. It was an ill omen.

On the other hand, the police chief of the district seemed a better person to Dhriti. He was polite to him on the phone. The police chief told Mr Mahapatra that he would come to meet Mr Mahapatra, collect the copy of the complaint from the tribal commission and personally deliver it to Mr Mahapatra. Mr Mahapatra was filled with praise and gratitude for this policeman, who still held the old-world values.

In the evening the police chief arrived, he delivered the complaint and requested him to read it only after he had left. They sipped whisky together and parted.

Mr Mahapatra was quite rattled by the events. With trembling hands he opened the envelope and focussed the lamplight on it. Reading the charge made out against him at this point of his life, his head reeled. A destitute tribal woman had sought compensation from Mr Mahapatra for bringing up his 'grandchild'. Her daughter, she claimed, was born out of liaison with Mr Mahapatra, then a widower DM at Bilaspur. The woman was his domestic servant. Her daughter had died leaving a child behind.

His intoxication vanished. Fortunately nothing had appeared in the newspapers. He immediately rang up the police chief. The police chief was apologetic on the telephone. He cut Mr Mahapatra short for the fear of being overheard. He again arrived at the circuit-house within a few minutes. Mr Mahapatra was disturbed by the charges.

'Sir, the CM (chief minister) Miss Rani Bai is a mad cap. She is a tribal feminist. She has been fighting for the rights of the tribal women. She has promised in her election manifesto to book the officials who had wronged them. It is now alleged that in the nineteen sixties and seventies a number of officers exploited the tribal maids. Those days this was an undeveloped area, and the officers never brought their families with them to stay here. Cohabitation with the beautiful tribal maids used to be the practice. Children were born to the tribal women, and the officers were transferred out. For sometime, they continued to make payments to them. Then all was forgotten, and hushed up. It was not something unusual those days. Rani Bai is raking up the past with her eyes on the election. These tribal women are now being incited by her.' Mr Mahapatra listened to the police chief with his eyes closed. He did not speak.

The police chief continued, 'Now when there are no outsiders, so called exploitation is over, their own menfolk do the same. But madam (the CM) doesn't dare to book them. She has closed her eyes to their own evil. Baba! It is their natural way of life, and they do not consider it exploitation. Marriage rituals are not known to them, they simply do not exist. They exchange a leaf or a flower and they are married till they part. They stay together and then move away irresponsibly. This hullabaloo is just a political stunt to garner votes.'

Mr Mahapatra who was listening to the young police chief quietly, interrupted, 'Eknath, you are telling me all this! My dear, I was a DM here.' Mr Mahapatra made a circle by joining the tip of his index finger to the tip of his thumb and shook it back and forth. 'I know them very well. They have absolutely no morals.' Mr Mahapatra opened the circle and gesticulated contemptuously, 'They lived like animals those days, ate raw worms. Many even did not even wear clothes. We civilised them, introduced them to clothes and cooked food. Now this is the reward being offered to us.' He thumped his breast. 'Hah! These beasts exchanged wild flowers for marriage.' Mr Mahapatra felt bitter and agitated. He stood up and walked to the supper table. He poured whisky into the glasses, mixed soda and ice and planted them on the small table between their chairs. Eknath picked up one. 'Cheers', they raised their glasses in the air.

'Sir, I will not blame the tribal people, it is their leaders who are feeding them strange ideas, and trying to introduce alien morality into their simple life.' Mr Mahapatra nodded in agreement.

Eknath continued with his speech, 'This operation has easy money in it for the tribal women. Who will not fall for it? Sir, I know it well, it is just a conspiracy to win elections. Hundreds of complaints are being lodged by the tribal women in the hope of extracting some money from their former employers. Some of them do not even know the name of the officer or his year of posting. I am sure none of these complaints will bear scrutiny in a court of law. It is all a political gimmick to make a fast buck. They are not bothered about the consequences and the fall out of this. It will destroy the uncomplicated tribal culture. That, they do not understand.'

Mr Mahapatra responded, 'You are right, my boy. This Rani Bai herself was a whore. She worked in the house of Gyan Joshi, my batch mate in the MP cadre. She would have ended as a domestic servant, had Joshi not helped her with her education. She became the first graduate among the tribal women. Later she joined the JJ Party and never looked back since. Having got the power, her repressed hatred for the upper class is finding expression. It is just an act of vindictiveness against her past masters. Sometimes I think that an excess of democracy is not good. It is like a sword in a monkey's hand.'

'I agree with you. Sir, don't you worry, all these are gimmicks and will disappear sooner than later,' Eknath reassured the agitated man.

'But I do not wish all this to go on. People like us have

nothing except a respectable name and honour. I would like to pay off this old woman and get out of the muck. Courts take long and your name comes to public light.'

'In that case I will fix it, Sir. It's done.'

'You mean it.'

'Yes Sir, I do.'

The two men stood up and shook hands; Eknath asked for Dhriti's leave.

'No, please sit down for a few more minutes.' Eknath sat down obediently. Mr Mahapatra poured another drink. Eknath knew that Mr Mahapatra could be helpful to him for his deputation to Delhi.

'What is this DM like?' Mr Mahapatra asked.

'A warped mind!' Eknath replied.

'Yes, he seems to be rather strange. I am old enough to be his father in the civil service. He has not called on me so far. Rather he refused to see me. Seems to be an arrogant fellow,' Mr Mahapatra complained.

'He is like that, Sir. He does not have good confidential reports from his seniors. He will have to pay for his misdemeanours,' the policeman concurred with Mr Mahapatra. 'They are likely to transfer him to the publication department.'

'Are you married, Eknath?' Mr Mahapatra asked.

'Yes Sir, with two children.' Eknath smiled.

Mr Mahapatra felt quite familiar with Eknath. Both were tipsy now.

'One thing I must confess. These days, not many Oriyas are found in the Indian Administrative Service, Sadananda is one of the few. If he is otherwise fine, I may overlook his temperament. I would like to meet his parents for my daughter. My daughter is now twenty-three.'

'You have experienced his behaviour, his looks are much worse. He is too uncouth for your family.'

'Eknath, the looks of men do not matter. It is self-confidence.

I too was dark and ugly. A good job made the difference. Do I still look ugly?' Mr Mahapatra cast a charmed glance on his own reflection in the life-size mirror on the opposite wall, and began combing his hair.

Eknath looked at Mr Mahapatra. There was truth in what Mr Mahapatra had said just now. 'There is no doubt that he holds a position of promise. Even with bad confidential reports he will draw the salary scale of a Secretary to the government before he retires. He will be paid in diamonds, if he gives up his job for a multinational. That way, I agree with you, Sir.' Eknath changed his position to suit Mr Mahapatra's will.

Mr Eknath located the woman. She lived in the servant's quarter of an officer. Policemen brought her. She was frightened, trembling at the sight of Eknath and Mr Mahapatra. Mr Mahapatra placed a bundle of fifty thousand rupees on the table. The old woman took it and put her thumb impression on the document held by the police chief.

She smiled humbly, 'Have you recognised me Sahib?'

Mr Mahapatra shook his head. He had no recollection of her.

'I worked in your house.' The toothless woman spoke.

Mr Mahapatra looked blankly at her. The woman folded her hands, and humbly said, 'Namaste Sahib,' and left the room.

'Bloody swine!' Mr Mahapatra ejaculated. He felt like a free man. The complaint was withdrawn, he sighed with relief.

'Sir, you are a real Casanova, women still fall for you. Didn't you observe her toothless grin? She still wanted to flirt with you. Beware, it is a dangerous country, Sir.' Eknath teased Mr Mahapatra.

'Bloody shit!' Mr Mahapatra drawled in a heavy Oriya accent. Both the men brayed like jackasses.

In the evening Mr Mahapatra rang the DM again. The DM congratulated him. He was polite and courteous this time. Eknath had already informed him.

'Sadananda, I am cleared, may I visit you at home now? I wish to see your bungalow where I lived for so many years.'

'Yes Sir, you are welcome for dinner tonight. I will come and fetch you. Sir, I am a vegetarian and do not serve alcoholic beverages. I hope this will not be inconvenient to you.'

'My son, do you think that I visit a person for food and beverages? I am an Oriya Brahmin with simple tastes. I wish to see your parents, who have produced a son like you.'

'You are welcome, Sir.'

Mr Mahapatra arranged a box of sweets and dry fruits each, in his brief case. He kept thc best pictures of his daughter. He organised his thoughts to make a marriage proposal for his daughter. Both the Mahapatras, travelled togethcr in the car for Sadananda's bungalow. 'Son, why haven't you married?' the senior Mahapatra inquired.

'Sir, I have not yet found the woman made for me.' Sadananda smiled.

'May I find one for you?'

'Please, do it, Sir.' Sadananda laughed.

'Can I speak to your father about it?'

'Sir, he died before my birth.'

'Sorry to hear that, Sada. May I meet your mother?'

'Yes of course.'

'My hats off to her for bringing up a son like you.' Dhriti drew Sadananda to his heart. It was really difficult to find an IAS officer of one's own caste.

Thc DM's bungalow was not far from the circuit-house, probably a seven-minute drive. That was the bungalow Dhriti had lived in as the DM then. It looked so different and smaller now. The brick walls were plastered and the roof was re-laid, tiles were replaced with cement sheets. The lawn appeared shrunken. The old trees were still there. But the spirit of the place felt different; it was humbler

The ice had melted. They chatted for long. Eknath had also

arrived with his spouse and children. Mr Mahapatra felt very cosy in the house. Eknath's wife admired the picture of his daughter. Mr Mahapatra passed a few more photographs to her. Sada appeared shy to look at the pictures. Mr Mahapatra suddenly remembered, he asked for Sada's mother who had not joined them. Sada shouted from his seat, 'Ma, come, see who has come.'

Mr Mahapatra pulled out the box of sweets and a photograph of his daughter to offer those to Sada's mother. She appeared at the door. Dhriti stood up to welcome her. She was a plump and elegant tribal woman. Dhriti was fazed to see her. He slowly tumbled down and asked for water. He perspired in the evening cold. The photograph fell on the floor.

He had exchanged a wild daisy with her in the same parlour.

□

Death Wish

'Brute! You have murdered my sister. I know this.'

'If you are so certain of my crime, go to the police,' Dhara barked.

'Slowly, but unfailingly law catches up with everybody, it spares no one. Wait, my dear. You will regret it for life.'

Sudha's body was still warm. Dhara and Devi laid her down on the ground like all Hindus do to a corpse. Sudha had suffered multi-organ failure. She had been in a coma for the last one week. Her death was imminent; it came as no surprise to Dhara. Devi wailed the loss of her sibling.

Sudha was a successful executive. She had climbed the ladder fast, and had become the chief executive of a television channel. Her husband did not do well in life. She had ignored a slippery knot in her breast for long. Till recently, it never troubled or pained her. Suddenly she found that the little thing had grown several times, it pulled her chest and skin to it. The day she went to the doctor it had burst open on the skin. The doctor labelled her as a case of advanced stage of cancer. Soon that spread to her liver and lungs. Her pain increased each passing day. Strong analgesics began losing their effect, so did her tolerance. One day she begged the doctor to put her to sleep. On each visit she asked for the same to the annoyance of the doctor. Her painful screams had become unbearable. Dhara then decided to help her out. He brought a bottle of arsenic powder and hid it in her clothes' shelf.

Devi was a spinster. She was a teacher in a primary school. On her meagre salary, she frugally managed her household. She had nothing to match her sister. To serve her ailing sister, she had quit her job, and moved to her sister's house. She had always suspected that Dhara had married Sudha only for her highly paid job, and her wealth. Her fear was confirmed when Dhara began neglecting his sick wife. He had become friendly with another woman in his office. One day, while cleaning the cupboard, Devi noticed a small bottle labelled 'arsenic sulphite', hidden in the clothes. She became curious, but did not touch it.

Now, the grim reality stared her in the face; her sister had died; the brother-in-law was hostile to her. Soon, after the ceremonies were over, Dhara thanked Devi for all she did for his wife. He suggested that it was the time for her to leave. Devi was shocked at her brother-in-law's indifference and selfishness. She was jobless and without a shelter. She sought some time.

Within a week of Sudha's death, Lalita moved in to console her lonely friend. Devi tried to reason with Dhara. She admonished him for his lack of respect for her dead sister. Dhara plainly refused to listen to her. 'Lalita will stay. You must find yourself a house at the earliest.'

'This is my sister's property. You shouldn't be talking to me like this. My sister earned all this wealth. I too have a moral right on this house,' Devi protested. She was annoyed at her brother-in-law, who showed no human concern. He appeared like a monster to her.

She had no choice but to leave her sister's house. Had her sister earned the house and wealth for Lalita? Devi brooded. She confided her problems and suspicions to a lawyer. On his advice, she filed a police complaint against Dhara.

'Inspector, she was a terminal case of cancer. Look at these documents.' Dhara spread open the hospital file.

'Shame on you! To facilitate your girlfriend you did not consider her ailment,' Devi lamented.

'It is very unusual Mr Dhara. Couldn't you wait for even a month before bringing in your girlfriend?' the inspector asked Dhara.

'Inspector, I will show you something. Please follow me,' Devi implored.

She removed the clothes and opened the cupboard. The bottle was still there. The inspector's eyes gleamed at the object. He wore his plastic gloves and held the bottle in his hand. He put on his spectacles, the bottle was half empty. He read the label, exclaiming loudly, 'Arsenic? What do you say to this Mr Dhara?' He carefully put the bottle in a zip-lock bag.

Dhara turned pale with fear. 'I was not aware of this. Perhaps my wife ended her pain with this. She had always asked the doctor to put her to sleep.' Dhara shivered.

'Who was her doctor?'

'Dr Yamuna Prasad of Sagam Hospital.'

The inspector carefully noted his statements in a tattered register.

'Madam, you should have informed us of your suspicion before the cremation of the body. Now we cannot confirm the cause of death. She was a cancer patient, her liver and kidneys had failed. There is no proof that she consumed arsenic or died of arsenic poisoning.' The inspector looked at Devi.

'To keep the memory of my one and only sibling alive I have collected her hair while preparing her body for cremation.'

The inspector was amazed at the wisdom of the woman.

'I am a graduate in chemistry.' Devi answered the curiosity in his eyes.

'We need hair with roots, only that would confirm if they are indeed your sister's and that they contain arsenic.'

'I had pulled out a bunch, if that helps you.'

'Wonderful!' The inspector was delighted at the possibility

of apprehending the murderer.

Devi removed her sister's relics from the refrigerator and gave them to the inspector. He carefully inspected the hair lock and placed a few in his plastic pouch. The rest he returned to Devi. She kissed them with moist eyes and replaced them in the silver casket.

Dhara was tried. The *vaidya* identified Dhara as the man who bought the poison to cure his own arthritis.

Dhara was sentenced for life for the crime of mercy-killing. Since the murderer is disinherited, the property went to Devi. Dhara became demoralised and lost his fire and temper. Lalita disappeared from his life, she never called him. The friends became indifferent. Cleaning floors and weaving carpets sustained his spirit in jail.

He was very surprised when Devi came to visit him in jail. He quietly sat on a stool gazing at the ground. Words did not come to him. Devi broke the ice, 'It saddens me to see you in this condition.'

'Have you married, Devi?' Dhara observed vermillion in her parting.

'Yes, don't you see that in my appearance?' she smiled.

'Who is the fortunate man?'

'Lalita's brother.'

Dhara was extremely surprised. 'Congratulations to both of you,' he said.

'Thank you.'

They sat quietly. Dhara contemplated on the irony of life.

The place was dark and cold, Devi shivered. 'It is always damp and cold here. Sunshine never warms this place,' Dhara complained.

'Dhara, whenever you need anything that I may help, ask me without hesitation.'

'Devi, you ought to believe me. I admit, I did buy arsenic

but I did not poison her. She found the bottle. Believe me, she committed suicide,' Dhara cried.

'How come only your fingerprints could be found on the bottle and not hers?' Devi accused him.

'I don't know about all that but, believe me, she killed herself.'

Devi wrapped her shawl around her neck and rose. It was time to go. She curved her lips to feign a smile and asked, 'Do you want to know the truth?'

'Yes.'

She contemplated for a while, and then with a straight face said, 'I fed her the poison.'

Dhara gaped at her. The guard blew his whistle, a warning to the visitors to leave.

'That was my sister's wish. Goodbye, Dhara.'

She walked to the exit. Dhara stood stupefied till the guard tapped his shoulder.

□

---

1. *Vaidya* refers to an Ayurvedic practitioner.

Promotion

An honest man in India is like an alligator at a village fair, a rarity and curiosity. Mr Shibo Prosad Banerjee was such a man. He was a senior officer of the Indian Railway Traffic Service. Amongst his colleagues and juniors, he was contemptuously referred to as Bunnerji Babu—of course behind his back.

He was a stickler for rules, read each word in a file with the sharpness of a clerk, and wrote copious notes frequent with 'ifs' and 'buts', and 'on the other hand'. The files containing his ambiguous notes and recommendations could never be processed by the higher-ups. Once he wrote on a file, the concerned matter generally ended before making any progress. That was his way to banish corruption from the railway life. Overruling his objections could cast aspersions even on Caesar's wife. His typical bureaucratic attitude to every matter constantly irritated his superiors. Public good also suffered sometimes, but he never let anything stir out of its turn. He often quoted I.S. Jauhar, his favourite actor, 'Bureaucracy is a game, in which the first one to move, loses.'

Dhong Singh of Mehrauli had taken over as the minister of railways. He was a no-nonsense man. He brooked no interference in his pleasures. He had served several upright officers right in the ministries he had headed. He was an experienced man.

Both, the bureaucrat and minister were aware of each other's reputation. Not to be intimidated, Mr Banerjee accepted a transfer from Delhi to Kolkata, farther than beyond the minister's influence—so he presumed.

Upto now, Mr Banerjee had crossed all the ladders with due speed. The moment to become the General Manager had arrived. He had no doubt that he would clear this as well, in the first shot. But this time, this minister had something else in mind.

The Chairman of the Railway Board asked Mr Banerjee to report to the minister. He reached the minister's office in time. He was duly made to wait for half a day. 'The minister is busy,' he was informed by the Secretary. However he was allowed in a couple of hours later. Dhong Singh beamed benignly, 'Welcome Bunnerjee Babu, come in, come in.' The minister welcomed him with great enthusiasm.

Mr Banerjee was stunned, how had the minister got to know this name? He always detested this address. The minister beckoned to a chair and asked him to sit down. Then, Dhong Singh put on his gold-rimmed, reading glasses; adjusted them over his nose-bridge pretending to read files. He scribbled here and there. Mr Banerjee could not help marvelling at his understanding and speed. After a quarter of an hour, seemingly tired of the exercise, Dhong Singh removed his spectacles, polished and examined the glasses, and then inserted them in a golden case. He slowly pushed the files aside, and called his attendant to bring tea for 'Bunnerjee Babu'.

'Bunnerjee Babu, sometimes I wonder, why I have entered politics. It is too murky for people like me. I wish I were a babu like you. You are not under any one. Whether you work or not, nobody can throw you out. With us, it is a twenty-four hour tension. Today I am here, tomorrow I don't know. In the last three years the PM has reshuffled his cabinet three times. He wants to see progress everywhere. Railways did not perform to his expectation; so, this time he asked me to set the rot right. (Please note: he was shunted out from the previous ministry on the charges of bribery and poor performance.) I don't know how long I will be here. The press is always against me. Anyhow, I wish to settle all the promotions before I leave, otherwise with a new incumbent, it may take another year. By the way, how many years are left for your retirement?'

'One and a half years, Sir,' Mr Banerjee blurted out. He had become anxious to hear of the possible delay in his promotion. It was already delayed by two years.

'People are full of praise for you. Honest officers like you are the backbone of the system. Though I am a politician, I like honest officers. But for them, the system would collapse as has happened at several other places, for example—the coal ministry.' The minister lampooned the Secretary of his former ministry, well-known for his integrity. 'You must get your promotion fast,' he declared with finality.

'Yes Sir.' Mr Banerjee concurred with the minister. He had no other choice.

'The panel for GM has three names. You are the seniormost. There is no reason why you should not become the GM. I do not wish to supercede you, but your corrupt junior—some Muslim fellow—has put tremendous pressure on my party president. He has offered twenty-five lakhs to the president for the elections. You know that the assembly elections are round the corner.' Then he became quiet for a while.

'What do you say to it?' the minister broke the silence.

'Sir, the president is your own mother. You may inform her of my honesty and unsound financial condition.'

The minister gave an enigmatic smile. 'I know, I know. You see, *Mataji* is a very different type of politician, an idealist of the old days. For her everybody is equal. No one is big or small, junior or senior, rich or poor, Brahmin or Sudra, Hindu or Muslim: all are equal in her eyes. Secularism is her creed.

'She does not listen to anyone, except her own soul. She sits on *satyagraha*[1] against the decisions of her own hand-picked working committee members. Innumerable times, she has performed self-purifying *anshans*[2], and fasts unto death. Finally everyone has had to veer around her will.

'You know, she had worked closely with Gandhiji. She was like a daughter to him. *Reason above Emotions*, is her mantra. It is all Gandhiji in her. You must have read in the newspaper, she turned out my own brother-in-law from the party.'

His eyes filled with reverence for *Mataji*. (Please note: Dhong Singh told only half the truth to Mr Banerjee; the brother-in-law had plotted against *Mataji's* son.).

'Sir!' The ground seemed to slip under the poor babu's feet. He sweated as his head reeled at what he heard at the end of his career.

Dhong Singh again politely warned, 'She worships secularism. She cannot compromise on it. Can she?' He vulgarly gesticulated, 'for nothing?'

Mr Banerjee nodded like a sheep in a slaughterhouse.

This pleased the minister. He took pity and said, 'Don't you worry Bunnerjee Babu. I know you have been an honest officer and haven't earned enough. I have made all arrangements on your behalf so that you do not suffer. I have ensured that you do not have to pay a single paisa from your own pocket. I have arranged a financier for you. You don't have even to return the money to him.' The minister smiled compassionately.

'I am a family man, husband of two wives, and father of thirteen children. I shouldn't have told you all this, but now everything is in the newspapers, thanks to the opposition,' Dhong Singh brutally admitted. 'This is the game of *sala*[3] Gidwaniji!' He spat a mouthful of betel juice into a spittoon, gargled with water and slurped tea. 'Please drink your tea. It is very good. It is from Darjeeling.'

He spoke with certain feeling now, 'I feel the pain of family men. I understand your problems. You have only to say yes. The rest, I will do, my party will do. I cannot offend *Mataji*, you understand? Now you may leave. Think about it, discuss it with your family, and let me know in a week's time.'

Mr Banerjee felt relieved as he left the room. He took an auto-rickshaw and returned to his guesthouse. Though he wrote obnoxious notes and always got away, he was really nervous about his promotion this time.

He discussed the matter with his wife. She rejected his suggestions outright, 'Leave it. Where shall we get the money to pay them? Mona is to be married in six months' time. That would cost us at least a good seven lakhs. Where shall we live after retirement, if you sell our Delhi flat?'

'The going rate of our flat is seventy-five lakhs. That will fetch us three such flats in Kolkata.' Mr Banerjee clarified. He disapproved of his wife's description of his helplessness.

'I will never live in Kolkata. Chittaranjan Park is best for us. All our children have grown up here.' His wife thoroughly discouraged Mr Banerjee.

'Even in Chittaranjan Park we may easily get another flat for fifty lakhs,' Mr Banerjee protested. 'Moreover, I do not have to pay a single penny from my own pocket. I just have to say, "Yes". That is all.'

The minister had given him a week. The husband and wife took a flight back to Kolkata the same evening. They found Daku *da*, a feared cadre-member of some political party, and Mihir Moulik on the staircase of their first storey government house. These Union leaders had never visited him at his home earlier. They actually had never dared to do such a thing. Mr Banerjee felt extremely annoyed to find these rogues waiting at the staircase of his house. He asked, 'What are you doing here? I am too tired; I have come straight from Delhi. See me in my office tomorrow,' and he walked up.

The duo followed him, 'Congratulations, Sir. This calls for a treat.'

'Treat for what?'

'Sir, we know all. Mantriji has offered you the position of GM.' Daku *da* then lowered his voice, twirled his fierce moustache, and said, 'Sir, we know all. You don't have to do a thing, just say yes to him and forget all about money matters. We will arrange everything without your knowledge.'

Mr Banerjee smiled wryly and asked, 'What will you expect in return?'

'Nothing, Sir. We expect honesty from you as ever.'

'That was why you have organised agitations for my transfer, danced on my table, and abused me all these days? I know you well. Now please go away.'

'The minister has asked us to help you out, Sir. He has said that you should not be disturbed. You should be allowed to continue. We will pay him the money on your behalf.

'He expects you to continue with your present responsibilities, and with the same spirit; only a few responsibilities will be transferred to your deputy.' Daku *da* spoke in a matter of fact way.

'What are the responsibilities that I am supposed to delegate to the Deputy GM?'

'Relief to passengers in case of accidents, auction of scraps, all such minor things. I will give you a complete list after you join the new assignment.'

'Oh I see! In traffic accidents! It is the station master's discretion to spend either five rupees or five hundred per passenger. He should be given a free hand with his discretion in such situations, isn't it?'

'Yes,' Daku *da* agreed.

'The scrap auction which now fetches the government crores of rupees should be handed over to the Deputy GM.'

'Yes,' Daku *da* growled.

'So that the revenue may again dip down to a few lakhs as it used to be before?' he sarcastically asked

'What do you mean?' Daku *da* raised his voice. He felt insulted.

'Thank you, rascals, I have already asked for my voluntary retirement. I had faxed my request before I left Delhi. You may go now.

□

---

1. Gandhian way of protest.
2. Fast.
3. A Hindi swear word.

The Forgery

Two brothers, Trevor and Robert Tressler lived happily in their family estate of ten acres and a beautiful bungalow over it. They were the sons of a Protestant priest who had made money from his business of moneylending and pawning, buying and selling property, and speculation. He had bought a decent property in the Christian Town, on the outskirts of Allahabad, now well set in the middle of the city.

Though darker than the natives, the priest Mr Tressler, claimed to be of Anglo-Indian descent. An ancestor came from Cornwall, a coastal town in southwest England, to Madras in seventeen-hundred and something. He baptised and married a local tribal woman in Coimbatore, produced numerous children, who in turn produced a hundred more. The clan spread all over India, if not Asia. They took up all sorts of occupations, with preference for teaching, nursing and priesthood.

The present-day Tresslers are proud of their English ancestry; they never identify themselves as native Christians. They always seek alliances with the local Anglo-Indians, who, in turn, deny them entry into their own caste.

Trevor was twenty years older than his little brother, Robert. He was a headmaster in a primary school. Trevor had married a fellow teacher, Anita, a woman of kind disposition and a devout Christian. The childless couple were like parents to Robert. They lived together in their ancestral home and shared their earnings, not much anyway, to meet monthly expenses. Though they owned a property worth millions of rupees today, they were always short of cash. They did not live the way the rich were supposed to live, but followed all the traditions of Christian Town—such as an alcoholic beverage before and after dinner, playing the guitar, singing English country songs and hymns in the local church, playing Tombola at the local fairs, and going to the dance floor on Saturday nights. However, they commuted on bikes, had no servants; they did their own cooking, washing and scrubbing. They grew seasonal crops and fruits on their field, and sold the produce in the market to make extra money.

It was a winter evening. Frost was expected at night. Robert supervised the watering of the wheat saplings. The sun was about to set in its own golden light. A beam through the trees illuminated a beautiful face and body. There was a young woman in the group of the farm workers. He was instantly drawn to her. He could not help ogling her. Mati was a vivacious young girl; she was fair skinned; she had thick, sensuous, pink lips, and well chiselled curves. She observed the gaze of the master, and instinctively retracted behind the others. But she took her cue. In a few days, she became Robert's trusted servant, to the resentment of the others of her ilk. The two would often disappear into the sugarcane thicket on the silly pretext of pruning and weeding.

Soon, the pregnant Mati and her mother moved into the Tresslers' house. The walls shrouded her existence in the world Instead of her, menopausal Anita was declared pregnant. She took six months' maternity leave. At the expected time, Anita was duly admitted to St Mary's Maternity Home, and came home with her bundle of joy, a baby girl. Mati fed her own breast milk to the baby for a few months. She was well compensated. Mrs Tressler found a suitable match for her. Mati was married off to a peasant in a remote village; she went away with him. The year was 1985.

Many things happened subsequently. Trevor retired the same

year, while Anita had another ten years to go. Robert finally married a pretty woman, Amanda, from the Anglo-Indian neighbourhood. And, in the same year, the newly weds migrated to Australia on the invitation of Amanda's expatriate uncle.

The next year, Trevor suddenly suffered a massive heart attack while tilling his field. He was admitted to the Nazereth Hospital in a critical condition.

'I do not wish to die and part from you,' he tearfully told his sobbing wife. 'Even if I die, I will never leave you, I will circumambulate around you,' he smiled with difficulty, coughed and passed into a coma. He died peacefully a few days later.

All by herself, heart-broken Anita managed the funeral. Robert could not come. Life turned harsher to her. It took a year for the government to release Trevor's pension to his widow. The field could not be cultivated that year as she hadn't enough to pay the labourers. She was left with her infant daughter, Fiona.

Robert came the next year with his wife and baby boy. They were shocked to see that Anita had aged and shrivelled, three-year-old Fiona looked pale and thin. The crops were not there on the field. The field had a few stubs of old crops, and wild shrubs. The fruit trees were leafless; ants had burrowed through the bark. The barricades were broken, barbed wires were stolen. Cows of unknown owners grazed on a few patches of wild grass which had survived.

Anita had no help. She left the baby with an uneducated woman in the neighbourhood while she cycled to her school. It was a pitiable sight.

Robert spoke to Anita, 'Anita, you have always been a loving mother to me. You must pardon me if I tell you that I am sad. I cannot bear this decline of our house, your health and the baby. Our green farm is dead, and the orchard is finished. Fiona looks pathetic. I cannot bear all this. Fiona is my daughter.'

'Oh I see, Fiona is your daughter! Were you not the one who wanted her killed before her birth to save your honour? I saved her, brought her up and now you are the father,' Anita bitterly retorted.

'Do not get me wrong. You are indeed her mother. I do not claim to be her owner or any such thing. I only want to help my family like everybody else in Australia does for his relatives,' Robert tried to cool her temper.

They argued and argued till Anita agreed to trust him with the child's welfare and education, and send her to Australia. Amanda was a good Christian, better than Robert. Anita relented on the promise that the child would be in regular touch with her, they would write about Fiona every other day, and they would visit her with the baby every year. With great pain in her heart the mother agreed to part from her only 'treasure and hope', as she would call her daughter. She too was ageing, she couldn't have met the aspirations and demands of a growing girl like younger mothers.

Reaching Sydney, Robert and Amanda forgot Anita and never wrote to her. Her letters to them remained unanswered. Anita retired in 1995. She was a lonely woman, confined to herself. That year, she received a Christmas card handwritten by her daughter. 'How beautiful Fiona's writing is. Each word is so clear,' she was fascinated. Fiona wrote, 'Dear Mom'. There was no end to her happiness when she read the word Mom. She added in her neat handwriting, 'I miss you. We will visit you in February, 1996. Uncle has even booked the tickets, for all four of us—Aunt, Andrew and himself. Dying to meet you. Lovingly, Fiona.'

Like every other night, Anita cried that night as well visualising Fiona, her only hope and treasure. Fiona must have grown tall; will she recognise her mother? Will she be as loving, as she was? The whole night, both positive and negative ideas crossed her mind. She was apprehensive. She remembered Trevor. Of course he was there in her mind, consoling her.

She cleaned and renovated the house, bought extra beddings. 'Fiona will sleep in my bed, Amanda, Robert and their boy will share another room. 'Oh God, I do not know how to thank you,' Anita cried.

Anita could not believe her eyes. Fiona was a very pretty child. She was grateful to Robert and Amanda. She could not have raised her like this. But she felt alarmed that Fiona, as she had expected, did not rush to her and cling. Though she called Anita mummy, she chose to stay close to Amanda, Robert and her little cousin. Anita felt very distressed. It was her decision to part from Fiona for the child's welfare; she had no reason to complain now. She sadly accepted this alienation. She told herself, 'Fiona should be happy. That is all that matters. And, she indeed is happy. A true mother lives in her child's happiness. It is my selfishness that is troubling me. I must feel happiness in her happiness.' She bowed to the Virgin on the altar, and smiled to herself.

Thank God, Robert paid no attention to the property this time. She was a poor manager. Poor people had encroached the land, they had raised sheds for themselves and their cattle. Their children played *gulli-danda* on it. Robert visited all his friends in the town. He was happy to meet his childhood friends and attend parties. Fiona stayed with her mother for a month. In no time, the day of parting came, it broke Anita's heart. Fiona left happily with her uncle and aunt saying pleasant things to Anita. She could feel the sense of relief in Fiona's voice. Instead of love, Fiona felt pity for the lonely old woman—her mummy. Anita realised this.

In a few days, after Robert's departure, she received a letter from Amar Das Law Firm: 'We are pleased to inform you that Mr Trevor Tressler has bequeathed his share in the property of the following description …., located in Christian Town, Allahabad, to his daughter Fiona Tressler; and also his monthly pension from the government of Uttar Pradesh to her. Till the time Miss Fiona Tressler is 18 years of age, Robert Tressler, the brother of Mr Trevor Tressler, will manage Miss Fiona's share of the property.

He will have full right to rent and sell the said property on behalf of Miss Fiona Tressler, till she is a minor.'

A copy of the will was attached, it was probated a few days earlier. Crestfallen Anita wept, 'How could you do this to me Trevor?'

When she regained her composure, she read the will again. It was not Trevor's signature. She felt Trevor stood there telling her the truth. 'That means Robert has forged your will,' she confirmed with Trevor.

'Yes indeed. Fight it out, I am here with you. Robert shouldn't have done this.'

'Hold my hands, Trevor,' she stretched her emaciated hands to an unseen presence. Trevor held them lovingly.

In the evening she rushed to Vinayak Saran, the famous advocate and Trevor's ex-student. He immediately recognised her and respectfully ushered her in. He patiently heard her and assured her of justice.

'Your fee, child?' Anita hesitatingly asked him.

'A guava from your tree; we used to steal those,' Vinayak laughed. 'And, of course...'

Anita held her breath to note his fee. 'Your blessings,' Vinayak completed his sentence dispelling her fear.

'It's all yours, child,' tearful Anita smiled.

The advocate contested the forged will. Anita wrote to Robert, 'Bring my daughter to the court here; I will hand over all that I have to Fiona, with my blessings. It does not matter if I have to spend my life in a charitable home for old people, beg, or die of penury and hunger. Bring her to court.'

The value of Trevor's share in the market was now over tens of lakhs of rupees. Land prices suddenly had shot up to the sky.

On the appointed date and time, Anita came to Kutchery, the district court, with Vinayak. She spotted Robert and Fiona standing near the car park. She rushed to Fiona and kissed her feverishly. Robert turned his face away. She took her away to a corner; the two could be seen talking.

'When did you arrive, Fiona? Where are you staying, dear?' the mother asked. 'You should have come straight to me,' she complained.

'We arrived yesterday, Mom. We are staying at the Barnett's Hotel. Uncle wanted it,' Fiona answered.

'My child, do you know what your uncle has done to me?'

'Mother, my father had willed his property to me. Uncle will manage the property on my behalf,' Fiona responded.

'My child the will is forged, it will deprive me of your father's meagre pension. I will get much less every month. I will not be able to survive,' Anita told Fiona.

'Mom, you are becoming older; people take advantage of you. Our property is being grabbed by cowherds and labourers. They have erected their shacks right under your nose; you couldn't do a thing about it. Uncle has decided to take care of the property and all of us,' Fiona reassured her.

'One of these cowherds was your wet-nurse. You will never understand many things,' Anita heaved a sigh; the odour of stale tea withered Fiona.

'I am deeply indebted to her for nourishing you when you were this little,' Anita smiled showing Fiona her length as an infant.

'I am sure, you and Father had amply compensated her then,' Fiona retorted.

'My child, Trevor is still to his pay his dues,' she said in anguish. After a while she again spoke, 'I do not wish to beg, my child. Your uncle is already the owner of half our estate and the house. He can sell it, or use it the way he wants. Why should he eye your father's share and pension, while I am alive? He is well settled in Australia. You must speak out against this injustice. You are a grown up girl, now.'

'There is no injustice, Mom. It is for the good of everybody.'

'I am your mother, I brought you into this world, you must trust me, Fiona,' Anita tried to persuade her.

'No, Mom, Uncle and Aunt have brought me up. Where were you when I was a small kid.'

'I was too poor and distraught to provide you the kind of upbringing and education that you have now. You are my only treasure and hope. For your welfare, I handed you to them, concealing my own feelings in wraps. I wept each day and night for you, my darling. You are such a pretty and educated girl now, Fiona.' Anita looked at Fiona with admiration in her eyes.

'Even poor people raise their children. I have seen so many women in tatters in this country, still clutching their babies. They work in farms, beg on the roadside. I still do not understand why you abandoned me, Mom?' Fiona began crying. Robert rushed to Fiona with scorn for Anita. He pulled Fiona away from Anita.

All of them parted, and followed their respective lawyers to the magistrate's court.

Anita, holding Trevor's hand, and Fiona accompanied by her uncle, stood in the opposite witness-boxes. The magistrate asked Anita to identify her daughter, and if she was satisfied. Robert smugly smiled.

Anita looked at Fiona, studied her face for sometime, and cried, 'Bring my daughter, Robert.'

'She is Fiona, your daughter.'

'No, she is not the Fiona you took to Australia.'

'She is indeed Fiona.' Robert reassured the court.

'Mom, I am Fiona. Don't you know me?' Fiona cried in amazement and disbelief.

Anita wept, 'No, my child, you are not my Fiona.' She began coughing furiously, took out her water bottle, and drank a little to clear her throat. The widow again faced Robert, 'Where is my Fiona, Robert?' she demanded in a harsh and manly voice. She coughed again.

Did he hear Trevor? A chill ran down Robert's spine. He

closed his eyes. 'Oh Jesus,' he drew the holy cross across his shoulders and head. With difficulty, he controlled his tremors from showing.

Vinayak Saran, the lawyer interrupted, 'My Honour, it is not difficult to find the truth these days. Why not order a blood test to match the DNAs of Mrs Tressler, and this girl who claims to be Fiona? Do you agree Fiona?'

'Yes Sir, by all means.' Fiona enthusiastically agreed.

The judge, too, nodded in agreement.

Still sweating, Robert feebly protested, citing ethics and offspring psychology. The judge overruled his objection.

During the next hearing, the sealed report was opened in the court, it read, 'Unrelated samples.' The judge looked sternly at Robert, 'She is not the same Fiona, Mr Tressler. Produce Fiona in this court. I want the Fiona Tressler born on September 25, 1985 to Mrs Anita Tressler at St Mary's Maternity Home, Allahabad. Or else, I order criminal proceedings against you,' the judge threatened.

'My Lord, you can see her birth and school certificates,'Robert tried to clarify.

'But this girl is not the same Fiona,' the judge overruled Robert.

The case dragged on, the police was given the task of finding Fiona. The Fiona, born to Anita, could not be traced.

Concluding his arguments, Vinayak Saran thundered in the court, 'Fiona is dead.' Pointing his finger at Robert he appealed, 'He has murdered her. Hang him, My Lord.'

□

---

1. *Gulli-danda*: A game popular in North India, where the player strikes with a wooden rod or twig and throws in the air a small, oval wooden piece tapering at both ends.

Incredible India

The President of Philippines bestowed the Ramon Magsaysay Award on him for his contribution to public hygiene and town cleanliness. He never thought of being awarded in such a manner in a foreign country; he was overwhelmed by his own importance. He tried to overcome his excitement by a show of excessive humility. Kripaluji shook hands with the woman president, and then suddenly doubled up to touch her feet, neatly wrapped in pink shoes, as he used to do always with the political bigwigs in India. Not to be seen wanting in courtesy, the surprised and confused President warmly reciprocated his gesture.

He returned with great fanfare. The Indian press gave a grand reception to him upon his return to India, of course, at his own expense. This sun of rural soil, known for his earthy wit and buffoonery, addressed a meeting at the Press Club of India.

'How did you feel receiving the award, Kripaluji?' a reporter asked.

'Indeed, very good. I have raised *Bharat-Mata's*[1] flag very very high on Manila's soil. Even the President of Philippines touched my feet for my accomplishments. I am the first Indian who have got this next-to-Nobel-Prize award.' Kripaluji boasted.

'First or hundredth?' Some reporter from the back-seats yelled, trying to correct him. Kripaluji appeared irritated at his ignorance.

'Was this your first foreign visit, Sir?' a reported asked.

'No, my plane touched Bangkok before landing in Manila.'

Everybody laughed. 'Don't you know that I had twice been to Singapore?' Kripaluji looked at the reporters with indignation.

'Is it true that you lived in jail there?'

'This is pure propaganda by the *sala*[2] opposition,' shouted a livid Kripaluji.

'Sir, this is a press conference, please do not use unparliamentary language here.' A man on the dais whispered in his ear.

'Lo, this is unparliamentary! Is it unparliamentary to call a scoundrel *sala*, own wife's real brother or cousin, Jyoti Babu? I feel it is perfectly Gandhian to be kind to your opponents,' Kripaluji addressed the next man on the dais, rather loudly.

The press corps hee-hawed at his witty riposte.

'Sir, can you please recount your contribution to public hygiene for which you won the Ramon Magsaysay Award?' an elderly man in the press gallery asked.

'Everything is published in foreign newspapers. I am no more a *desi*[3] news item. I work for raising India's honour and prestige in foreign countries. The foreign dignitaries touch my feet, and my own people ask questions about my achievements; how ridiculous? I am a humble man, cannot keep praising myself.'

The audience roared with laughter. Then he turned to an associate seated behind him on the dais, 'Netram Babu[4], please tell these people about me.'

Netramji[5], a coherent man, explained Kripaluji's contribution in improving sanitation in Tirana. Tirana was rated as the cleanest town of India these days.

Later, Netram Babu announced, 'All the pressmen and reporters can collect news clips on Kripaluji after the dinner. You will find all the details about our Mayor Sahib in it.'

Kripaluji folded his hands, rose briskly and left the podium.

Kripaluji, now a mayor, rose to this position from that of a small time *goonda*[6] in the township of Tirana in Bimaru Pradesh. He had once been deported from the town for a year, but he was allowed back on the promise of good behaviour. He tried his hands at various vocations including contractual construction, trading of potatoes, and secretly, *thugee*[7] as well. He worked in partnership with his trucker friend, Badmas Singh, now an MLA[8].

Kripaluji had become an influential municipal corporator of his town, and was appointed the corporator-in-charge of road maintenance. It was quite a profitable charge. He siphoned off enough to build a second house for himself. Still he had enough cash left with him; and now the time came to make a foreign trip and break the monotony of his colourless, hard life in Tirana.

The travel agent organised their travel to Singapore. It was their first air journey. Fastened in a seatbelt by a steward, they felt like a cow tied to the stake. Suppressing their natural urges, they awkwardly sat stiff all the while in the aircraft. It was quite frightful. They kept watching their amused neighbours to take cues in aircraft etiquette. All the way, they recited *Hanuman Chalisa*[9] for their safety. In a few hours, Kripalu and Badmas landed in Singapore. They had to be helped out of their seatbelts.

They could not believe their eyes that they were on the earth—no mud, no dust, no familiar smell. Singapore's Changi International Airport is the cleanest and most aesthetic port of the world. They had never seen such cleanliness, and decided to move around and inspect the whole complex before taking a trip out to the city and their hotel. Not a spot with betel-spit mark! Not a housefly around! They felt it was some heaven. They abused the Indian sense of cleanliness. 'Rascals in India spit everywhere. Look here, Brother. It is a heaven on earth,' exclaimed Kripaluji. Badmas added his bit and agreed.

They went to a duty-free liquor shop and recognised the bottles of Chivas Regal with glee. They bought a bottle. It was so cheap there. Both finished the bottle in no time; they had forgotten about the taxi waiting outside for them.

Kripaluji sniffed the mouth of Badmas, it stank of alcohol. He dutifully informed him.

'Lets chew a pinch of tobacco, then smoke a *bidi*[10]. No one would be able to get the smell of alcohol,' Badmas suggested adjusting the folds of his *dhoti*[11].

'You are an evil genius,' Kripaluji winked drawing a small

pouch of scented tobacco, Kha-Ja-Khaini, from his pocket. Both sniffed it and tapped out the contents in their mouths. They left the empty pouch on the seat, and coolly walked away to the Butterfly Garden and admired the butterflies, and insect-eating pitcher plants. In a short while their cheeks swelled with saliva. More was pouring in and they did not have further room inside their mouths. They could not open their mouths for the fear of spilling the saliva on floor. Swallowing it was dangerous; they needed to spit it out urgently. They looked around for sometime and not finding anyone in view, Badmas spat on the undergrowth of a plant and gestured Kripaluji to follow suit. Kripaluji looked around, no one looked in their direction; he carefully lifted the leaf-lid of a pitcher plant and deposited his spit in the pitcher over a decaying wasp, and softly replaced the leaf-lid as if nothing had happened. They smiled at each other triumphantly. No one had found them spitting. Now was the time for a smoke. They came out of the Butterfly Garden, and walked into the Mall area. They found several smokers at a particular place. They went to one of them and asked in their fractured English for a lighter. They unwrapped and lit their *bidis*, blew enormous columns of smoke like steam engines, and moved out. They loitered inside a mall for a while. Alcohol in their system provoked them.

They discovered, and walked into the toilet. Their eyes opened wide. It was unbelievable that people could excrete in such beautiful and clean places. They were simply amazed. With great difficulty they could restrain their urge to evacuate themselves outside these clean ceramic vases. Had it been India, they would definitely have peed outside, and saved the clean, glistening, pearl-white pots. But there, since many people released themselves exactly inside those bowls; the two followed, against their own conscience. They again came out wondering about the strange place.

Two baton-wielding men in blue uniforms, apparently policemen, came charging towards them, and threatened the duo to follow. Authority in their voices was intimidating. The two ridiculed the strange manner of policemen's speech, at the same time they now felt scared. However, the two threatened to rape the mothers and sisters of all the Singaporeans, albeit in subdued tones, and in Hindi, lest the policemen understood them.

They were pushed to a room where a big fat man sat across a wide table. He looked tersely at them. A policeman brought out a funnel and thrust that over their mouths, and shouted, 'Alcohol!' The senior man looked at another policeman, who came forward and swiftly handcuffed both of them. Now they were really terrified. They were pushed, and driven out in a police vehicle to another place. There, an officer menacingly spoke to them in broken Hindi. 'Why did you spit in the Butterfly Garden? Why did you leave your tobacco packet on the seat of the lounge, and why were you smoking in a no-smoking zone?'

The two aggressively denied all the charges, swore on their honour till a replay of their actions, they had so forcefully denied, was projected on the wall. They marvelled at the deviousness of the police.

The joy of visiting Singapore turned into a terror. The very next day they were caned on their buttocks and calves. They were put in a jail for three months for a list of offences, including the natural activities—littering and spitting.

The jail was no less clean. They were struck by the tidiness. They were given the job to clean the floors and toilets. Though they regretted not seeing the city and their inability to shop, for which they had come; they enjoyed their job.

Immediately after their jail term was over, they were put on a flight to Kolkata. From there, they took a train to reach home, Tirana.

Tirana was in the grip of pestilence when the two men arrived home. The scourge had killed over a hundred people. The city was terrorised, people were fleeing out of the city to other towns and villages. A cleaning drive was in full swing. The sanitary workers quarrelled with their supervisors in the Corporation for unnecessary work load of cleaning the piles of garbage from each street, and killing rats. They felt that it was sheer exploitation. How could garbage and rats cause plague? They were there even last year, and the year before, and nothing had ever happened, they argued. Many of them ran away or took long leave to avoid the work and scourge.

Kripaluji's family physician confirmed the fact that the disease had spread out of the garbage dumps where the rats had bred in large numbers. The rodents had now spread all over the drains, streets and houses. He hated filth for the first time. This was the beginning of a new chapter in the corporator's life.

Kripaluji had been a corporator for long. He had always harboured the ambition of becoming the mayor of Tirana. Now he saw the opportunity falling into his lap without much ado. The plague was a blessing in disguise. The scourge abated in due course, just before the elections. The ruling party was routed, Kripaluji's party won. Kripaluji took over as the new mayor of Tirana.

The secret of his victory was the support of the sanitary workers who canvassed for him wholeheartedly, day and night. Kripaluji had promised a foreign trip and training to all the 350 sanitary workers of the corporation in his election manifesto.

The new mayor forced the corporation to sanction return-airfare to Singapore for all the workers. He promised the workers the local hospitality in Singapore from his own, personal resources.

All his supporters were sent to Singapore in small groups. Each of them, without an exception, landed in jail and returned in three months with an excellent training in his trade. Tirana became the cleanest city of not only Bimaru Pradesh, but of India. The rest is history; you have read it already.

---

1. *Bharat Mata*: Mother India.
2. *Sala*: Wife's brother, also a swear word in Hindi suggesting an obscene relationship with the abused's sister.
3. *Desi*: Local.

4 & 5. These suffixes after a name are a mark of respect.

6. *Goonda*: A ruffian or mugger.
7. *Thugee*: Cheating and Fraud.
8. MLA: Member of Legislative Assembly of a state within India.
9. *Hanuman Chalisa*: Forty verses in praise of the monkey god, Lord Hanuman. Recitation of the *Chalisa* supposedly saves from all the miseries.
10. It is a local cigarette made by wrapping tobacco in a leaf.
11. *Dhoti*: A wide loin cloth wrapped around the limbs by villagers and politicians.

□□□